Amy Cross is the author of more than 100 horror, paranormal, fantasy and thriller novels.

THE
HORROR
OF
BRIARWYCH
CHURCH

AMY CROSS

This collected edition
first published by Dark Season Books,
United Kingdom, 2018

ISBN: 9781790805549

Also available in e-book format.

www.amycross.com

CONTENTS

THE
HORROR
OF
BRIARWYCH
CHURCH

CHAPTER ONE
MARK

"OH GREAT, THERE'S A church here. What a relief."

Turning, I look out the car window and see that Kerry's right. A church spire is rising up from behind the trees. As the car slowly navigates the tight bend in the heart of the village, I watch the spire for a moment before looking back down at my phone.

"Hey dumb-ass, did you hear what I said?"

Suddenly she punches me hard in the leg.

"Stop that," I mutter, pulling away slightly, even though I know there's no point. She can still easily reach me from the other side of Mrs. Trevor's back seat.

"Well why didn't you answer?" Kerry asks.

"It's rude not to answer someone when they talk to you, you know. Didn't your parents teach you any manners?"

I turn and glare at her.

"Oh right," she adds with a grin, "I forgot about the whole orphan thing." She leans over and nudges my shoulder with a closed fist. "We orphans have to stick together, right? I'm sure someone said something like that once, in one of those crappy motivational seminars they made us go to."

"You two aren't fighting back there, are you?" Mrs. Trevor asks from the driver's seat. "Please, tell me that two fifteen-year-olds can handle a two-hour car journey without resorting to fisticuffs."

"Mark started it," Kerry replies brattily. "He was being rude."

"She hit me!" I point out.

"He didn't reply to my comment about how beautiful Bumblewych looks," Kerry adds, "so I thought maybe he was unconscious, or even that something was wrong. I wanted to wake him up, but only because I care. Really, I was being kind."

"We're about two minutes from the house," Mrs. Trevor replies, sounding a little tired, "so let's just try to be in a good mood when we get there, yeah? And it's Briarwych, Kerry. Not Bumblewych. Your new home is called Briarwych."

***

"It smells funny here," Kerry says as soon as she's out of the car. "It smells really weird. Mrs. Trevor, what's that weird smell?"

"It's probably the lack of pollution," Mrs. Trevor replies, forcing a smile as she slams her door shut. "Have you ever left the limits of the M25, Kerry?"

"I think I like how pollution smells," Kerry says, scrunching her nose. "All this fresh air smells like cows' arses to me. I saw some cows a few miles back, on the road coming here. Did you know that cows are constantly farting? They just shit and fart and -"

"Quiet!" Mrs. Trevor hisses, turning to her. "We talked about this last night, you just have to get used to a different way of life out here, that's all. It's going to be a big change for both of you, but you're both more than capable of it. And believe it or not, you might actually grow to like the place if you approach your time here with the correct attitude."

"How many people get stabbed here each year?" Kerry asks.

"That's not funny, Kerry."

"It's a serious question!"

Sighing, I turn just as I hear a door opening nearby, and I spot a middle-aged woman coming out from one of the cottages, wearing an apron. I can immediately tell that she seems nervous. She smiles briefly at me as she wipes her hands on the apron's front, and then she fumbles to open the gate that opens out onto the street. Somehow she manages to miss the little bar that slides across. I don't think I've ever seen anyone so nervous in my whole life.

"Is it more than ten a year?" Kerry asks, clearly still thinking that she's hilarious. "Is it less than ten?"

"You must be Caroline Neill," Mrs. Trevor says, walking over and shaking the nervous-looking woman's hand. "Maxine Trevor, we spoke on the phone."

"Welcome to Briarwych," this Caroline Neill woman says, glancing briefly at me and at Kerry before turning to Mrs. Trevor again. "How was your journey?"

"Long," Mrs. Trevor says. "Traffic, you know?"

As she speaks, a man emerges from the cottage. He looks a little older than the woman, but I think he's her husband. I don't know why, I just think they look like they go together well. You can tell that about people sometimes.

"And let me introduce your two new arrivals," Mrs. Trevor continues, turning and gesturing toward Kerry and Me. "Caroline and Brian Neill, please meet Ms. Kerry Lawrence and

Mr. Mark Duffley."

"Do many people get stabbed to death here in Bowelwych?" Kerry asks them with a grin. "What about gang killings?"

***

"Normal TV's shit," Kerry says, sounding bored as she continues to flick through the channels, and as the others talk in the kitchen. "Why do they show so much shit?"

Trying to ignore her, I stare out the window. Afternoon is slowly turning to evening and the tops of the trees are swaying slightly. Beyond the trees, the spire of the church stands silhouetted against the sky, looking very lonely as it towers above the rest of this little town. Or village, I suppose. Yeah, I guess Briarwych must be a village. And that church looks wrong somehow, like it's standing out from everything else. Almost like it's dead.

"What the fuck are you doing?" Kerry asks.

Turning, I see that she's staring at me from the sofa. She's fiddling with a pack of post-it notes she found on the table, and she has her feet up on one of the arms, like she feels right at home already. Either that, or she's trying to make some stupid point.

"Nothing," I reply.

"You look like a moron, the way you're

looking out that window. There's literally nothing out there to look *at*."

"I was just looking at the church."

"Oh, so *now* you have something to say about the church, after *I* pointed it out to you?"

"I was just wondering why it's empty," I tell her. "It seems weird to have a church and not to use it."

"Who says it's not used?"

"It's abandoned," I point out.

"How the fuck do you know?"

"Well..."

Turning back to look at the spire, I suddenly realize that she's got a point. The spire is all I've seen of the church, but for some reason I just assumed that the building has been left abandoned and unused. I guess that's just the vibe I got from staring at the spire, but I'm probably wrong. It's probably used heaps. I always jump to conclusions like that about things, and about people too. I reckon I'm right about the church, though. Something about that spire just looks like no-one's been into that place for years. Maybe even decades.

Suddenly I hear the kitchen door open, and Mr. and Mrs. Neill come through, followed by Mrs. Trevor. They've been laughing about something.

"So, then," Mrs. Trevor says with a faint smile, as she looks first at Kerry and then at me, "this is where I leave you guys, for now. I've told

Caroline and Brian that you're both very good kids, and that you won't cause any trouble during this month-long trial residency. I've also told them that they're very brave for taking two of you on at once but, well, they're old-hands when it comes to fostering and I have no doubt that they'll manage just fine. You are, however, their first guests from London. They usually foster children from the local area, but I told them not to be scared of you two big-city high-rollers. Just try not to cause trouble, though, okay?"

She turns to Kerry.

"And be nice," she adds.

"It's so nice to meet you both," Caroline says, stepping forward. She still seems nervous, and she's still wearing that apron. "I think you're really going to like Briarwych. It's probably a little different to what you're used to, but there's actually a lot to do around here. We're not quite as sleepy as we might look."

"Thank you for having us," I reply, remembering what Gran used to tell me about being polite to strangers. "It looks really nice here."

I turn to Kerry.

She's staring at the TV again, and after a moment she changes the channel.

"Kerry," Mrs. Trevor says, "do you have anything you'd like to say?"

"Not particularly," Kerry mutters as the

images flash on the screen, casting a faint glow across her face.

"The forest stretches out for miles and miles," Brian Neill says, clearly trying to get a friendly conversation going. "I actually have a couple of unused BMX bikes that are in good condition, so I was thinking I could show you some parts of the local area. If either of you enjoy that kind of thing, there are some great tracks that are really worth exploring."

"That sounds cool," I tell him, and to be honest I feel a little sorry for him. He's trying so hard. His wife is, too. I guess it's important to try to meet them halfway. "I'd like to go out on a bike some time."

"It's hilly," he warns me. "You need to be in good shape."

"I reckon I am," I reply, and I smile to try to let him know that I'm being friendly. "I'm up for a challenge, anyway."

"I told you you'd like it here," Mrs. Trevor says. "Once we get the one-month trial residency out of the way, we can think about making it permanent if everyone's happy."

"Cool," I say, nodding to show that I understand. I turn to Caroline Neill. "You have a really nice home here. It's just a bit different to what I'm used to in London, that's all."

"Hang on." She steps closer and reaches

past me, before removing a pink post-it note from my back.

Sighing, I see that the word 'Wanker' has been scribbled on the note, and I turn to see that Kerry's grinning.

"Well," Caroline mutters, "I'm sure things will calm down soon enough."

"It smells of shit outside," Kerry says suddenly, still staring at the screen as she flicks aimlessly from channel to channel. "How can anyone live in a place that smells of shit?"

I don't know why she always has to be so snarky. Sometimes I look at Kerry and I really, honestly wonder what's going on inside her head.

CHAPTER TWO
KERRY

HOLDING MY T-SHIRT UP with my left hand, I use a finger on my right hand to trace the pale, rippled lines that criss-cross the side of my belly. As I do so, I stare at the reflection of the scar in the bathroom mirror, and I think back to that night.

"Fucking bitch!" Carl yelled as he fell on me and forced the blade into my body. "How do you like that, you gobby fucking cow?"

I remember the shock. After all the threats, which had been going on for weeks, he'd finally done it. Up until that moment, I thought it was all just banter, that he understood I was only winding him up for a laugh. And then he'd boiled over or something and he's lost it for a few seconds, and in those seconds he stabbed me eight times. What was it that the doctor said? That I was lucky to have survived? That I was about thirty seconds from death when the paramedics arrived?

I didn't think I was going to make it, not at first. Carl ran away after realizing what he'd done, and I only made it because his mate Jack rang the ambulance anonymously. He ran too, though, and for a while I was just slumped on the ground in that alley, in complete darkness, unable to do anything except feel my blood soaking out into my jeans. For a few minutes there, I really, truly thought I was going to die. I swear, for the rest of my life I'll always remember that feeling of being on the ground and having my life drain away from me. I don't just mean the blood. It was as if my soul was just emptying itself. I was so weak, and so scared.

Two years later, all that's left are these scars.

"Fuck you, Carl," I mutter under my breath. "I hope you're enjoying prison."

Suddenly someone tries to open the bathroom door, and I panic as I drop my t-shirt's front and look over my shoulder. Fortunately I remembered to lock the door, but the handle still turns a couple more times, as if someone out there doesn't quite understand the concept of privacy. Or locks.

"Are you still in there?" Mark asks. "You've been in that bathroom for ages."

"I'll be out soon," I tell him. "Go and piss in

the garden if it's that urgent."

"How long will you be?"

"Not long." I wait for him to go away, but I can tell that he's still out there. "I'm having my period."

Again I wait, and this time I hear a sigh before he slinks back to his room.

Good. I got rid of him.

Turning back to look at the mirror, I lift my t-shirt again and take another look at the scars. I know I spend way too much time looking at them, but they're pretty mesmerizing. They look like roads from above, and I smile as I imagine tiny little people driving around and living their lives down there. I wonder what kind of people they'd be, living on streets made out of my scars? For some reason I imagine them being weird little lumpy clay people with no arms, wobbling around in a weird, fleshy city. And because they had no arms, they'd have to be nice to each other.

***

"It must feel like you've moved to another planet."

Startled, I turn to see Caroline Neill standing in the doorway. Has she been watching me the whole time, while I've been getting myself a glass of water?

"Dunno," I reply, looking back down at the

glass as I finish filling it and turn the tap off. "I've never moved to another planet, so I've got nothing to compare it to, have I?"

"I've been to London three times in my life," she continues, "and I got a migraine each time. I know that probably sounds pathetic to you, but a place like London is just too big and too crowded. There was so much noise, and when I blew my nose for days after I had all this black stuff come out. Soot, I suppose, or some particles from the air."

"Gross," I say, and I can't help wondering why she's telling me this stuff. I pause, before drinking from the glass.

"Maxine tells me that you're into art," Caroline continues, "but she didn't really tell me what you do."

"Nothing."

"She told me that you're really good at drawing."

I shrug my shoulders. Why is she asking this stuff?

"I don't know what you like to draw," she says, "but there's some very pretty scenery around here. If you're into landscapes, you can't go wrong if you head up to Mayford Hill and look at the view from there. It's out near the abandoned RAF base. Honestly, the light out there is exceptional."

"Right," I mutter, as I put the glass back down and head to the door. "Night."

"Maybe we could take a walk out there tomorrow?" she suggests.

"How far is it?"

"About three miles."

"I'm not walking three miles." I slip past her and head out into the hallway. "My legs'd fall off."

"Then maybe another -"

"I'm just gonna chill tomorrow," I add, turning to her. "Is that allowed? Are people allowed to chill in the countryside? I thought that was the whole point of coming out here?"

"Of course. You need to adjust to your new surroundings, I understand that. Maybe you can explore with your friend."

"What friend?"

"Well, Mark seems -"

"Mark's not my friend," I tell her. "I only met him a few weeks ago, when I got shifted to the new home before coming here. He's alright, I don't hate him or anything. He's a bit weird, but I don't really hang out with him. He does things like stare out the window at the pointy bits of churches, that sort of thing. Like I said, he's weird."

"Was he looking out at our church?" she asks.

"He's a bit of a freak."

With that, I turn to go upstairs.

"Actually," Caroline says suddenly, "that's one place I wouldn't bother exploring."

I stop and glance back down at her.

"The church, I mean," she continues. "And the cemetery, too. It's very old and it's been abandoned for a long time, and it's not particularly safe. So if you *do* go out exploring tomorrow, please steer clear of the church, okay?" She pauses, watching me as if she's keen for me to tell her that I understand. "Okay, Kerry?"

"Are you worried some bits of stone are gonna fall off the roof and brain me?" I ask.

"There's really nothing there except overgrown weeds and loose brickwork and silence," she replies. "It's very boring, so please just promise me that you won't go into the cemetery or near the church. Do we have a deal?"

"What if I just want to take a look?" I ask, feeling as if she's warning me off the place.

"There really is so much to do here in Briarwych," she continues. "If you like, we can go to the corner-shop and see what art supplies they have. I doubt it's a very good selection, but they should at least have some pens and drawing pads. That's something to be getting on with, isn't it?"

"I'm alright," I reply. "Like I said, I'm just gonna chill tomorrow. But you guys should seriously think about getting some new channels on your telly, 'cause you've only got, like, twenty or something. That's mental."

"I'll look into it."

I pause, before turning and making my way up the stairs. Caroline says goodnight as I go, but by the time I'm at the top I figure she wouldn't even hear me if I replied. I don't really want to see her again until breakfast in the morning, and I might even skip that. During our little meeting about the house rules earlier, she told us what time breakfast's going to be served, but it kind of went in one ear and out the other. As I head to my room, I figure that tomorrow I'm just going to sleep in. The more I sleep, the faster this month is going to pass.

Stopping at the door, I realize I can hear voices coming from one of the other rooms. I hesitate, before going over and looking into what turns out to be some kind of makeshift office. To my surprise, Brian Neill and Mark are looking at some stupid toy cars.

"Oh hey, Kerry," Brian says when he spots me, "please, come in. I was just showing Mark my rather silly collection of die-cast Formula One cars."

"Okay," I reply, raising a skeptical eyebrow. "Whatever keeps you happy."

"He's got every single car since the 1996 season," Mark tells me. "Isn't that crazy?"

"Crazy's not *quite* the word I'd use," I say, as I look at all the different-colored little cars that are laid out on shelves lining the walls of the room. It's like being in a child's bedroom, except Brian's supposed to be a grown-ass man. "Are they worth anything?"

"Not much," Brian replies. "A few of them are slightly rare, but no-one's ever going to pay a lot of money for a 1996 Lavaggi Minardi."

"Whatever that is," I say, putting on a big, fake smile. "Nice to see you boys are having fun, though. Don't let me disturb you."

Stepping back, I stop on the landing for a moment and listen as they start talking again. I can't decide whether Mark's a massive suck-up, or whether he's actually interested in Brian and his stupid collection of toy cars. Anyway, I guess it doesn't matter, because I probably won't be sticking around for long enough to have to listen to much more of their dumb chatter. Heading back to my room, I've already pretty much decided that I'll be out of here before the month's up, and after a moment I stop and look back toward the other door, and I listen again to the sound of them talking. If I could figure out which of those toy cars I can sell, I might take a few when I go back to London. That way I can get a few quid and get on my feet, and after that I won't ever need help again, not from anyone.

After stepping into my room, I take care to push the door shut. There's no way I'm ready to go to sleep, though. Like they say, there's plenty of time to sleep when you're dead. I've got a much better idea about what to do tonight.

CHAPTER THREE
MARK

"HUH? WHAT?"

Suddenly realizing that something's bumping against my shoulder in the darkness, I open my eyes and turn to see a figure leaning over my bed.

Startled, I roll onto my back, and then I realize that Kerry has snuck into my room.

"Keep your voice down," she whispers. "It's two in the morning and I'm going out. You want to come with?"

"We're not allowed out in the night," I remind her.

"I don't recall anyone telling us that."

"I'm pretty sure it was implied."

"Who gives a shit? Anyway, we'll be back

before anyone knows we're gone. Come on, I've got a really cool idea. I'm only inviting you along because I feel sorry for you."

"Where are you going?" I ask.

"Where do you think?" she replies, before turning to look at the window.

Following her gaze, I see that she must have opened the curtains before she woke me up. For a moment, all I see is darkness outside, but then I realize I can just about see the spire of the church.

***

"This is stupid!" I mutter as we make our way along the steep road that winds up toward the church. "They're going to know that we left the house! I can't believe we even got out on our first night!"

"Everyone has to sleep sometime," she replies, sounding a little out of breath up ahead. "Anyway, it's that Caroline woman's fault, she practically *dared* me to come out here. Seriously, she must have known that by saying that, she was only making it definite that I'd come and poke around. If she'd just not said anything, I wouldn't even have cared about some stupid, abandoned old church."

"Is it really abandoned?" I ask, as she stops at the gate and I hurry to join her.

Looking through at the cemetery, I see that

the grass is massively overgrown. I can see the tops of tombstones poking out and gleaming in the moonlight, but the church itself is a little further off and for a moment I can't help but stare at the dark windows. Something about this place makes me feel even colder than I felt a few minutes ago when we crept out of the house. And as I continue to look at the windows, I can't shake the strangest feeling that somehow they're staring back at us.

"Looks like you were right when you said nobody comes here," Kerry says, and now I can see her breath in the cold night air. "Lucky guess, huh? By the way, have you still not checked your shoulder?"

"Huh?"

Reaching over my shoulder, I sigh as I find another post-it note. Taking a look, I see that it says 'Still a Wanker' in thick letters.

"Very funny," I mutter.

"What's wrong, Mark? Not got a sense of humor?"

With that, she reaches down to open the creaking old gate, only to find that a thick chain has been wrapped in place to keep it shut.

"Seriously?" she says, sounding amused by the situation. She tries a couple more times, causing a clanging sound to ring out like a bell. "Don't these doofuses know anything about basic human psychology? The more you try to stop people going somewhere, the more they're gonna go there."

"Hey, stop," I say, grabbing her hand and pulling it away so she doesn't keep trying the gate. "You're going to wake someone up."

"Don't touch me!" she snaps, pulling away.

"Sorry, but you were making a lot of noise!"

"Well, I'm getting in here, whether you like it or not," she replies, before stepping past me and then clambering over the low stone wall. "Why even bother locking the gate, when it's so easy to go in anyway?"

"They probably trust people."

"Losers."

"Do we have to do this now?" I ask. My teeth are almost chattering. "Can't we come back in the daytime?"

"*You* don't have to do anything at all," she says, before dropping over the wall and then turning to grin at me in the moonlight. "I only invited you along because I felt sorry for you. I don't need anyone here, though, so feel free to go back to bed like a good little boy. Just don't make a noise and don't snitch on me, or I'll make you fucking regret it, okay?"

She turns and starts picking her way through the overgrown grass and weeds.

I open my mouth to call after her, to tell her yet again that this is dumb, but then I realize that there's no point. She always seems determined to do the opposite of what anyone tells her, and I'm too tired and too cold to waste any more energy trying to babysit someone who's so obstinate. I watch for a moment as she continues to make her way toward the church, and then I turn to go back to the cottage. I am so not in the mood for this nonsense.

At the last moment, however, my hand brushes against the cold cemetery wall, and I feel a sudden shudder rush through my chest. Almost as if something grabbed my shoulder, I turn and look back at Kerry as she gets closer and closer to the large, dark church. She's getting harder and harder to see as she makes her way through the overgrown grass and bushes, and I lose sight of her for a few seconds. When I manage to spot her again, she suddenly looks so small against the huge bulk of the church.

And still those dark windows stare out at us.

In that instant, I suddenly feel deeply, deeply scared for her, as if on some hidden level I know that something's wrong. I can't shake the overwhelming sense that somehow there's something waiting in there, that Kerry's bumbling straight toward something she doesn't understand.

"Hey, come back!" I call out, barely managing to raise my voice. She's too far away, though, so I know I only have one option. "Damn it, Kerry!"

Even though I just want to get out of here, I

climb over the wall and drop down the other side. As soon as I've crossed the threshold of the cemetery, my sense of dread increases massively, and I swear I can feel something pressing on my chest. The tall grass is rustling all around me in a gentle wind, and I have to peer past several leaning old gravestones before I'm able to spot Kerry approaching the side of the church. She makes her way past one of the windows, and I can feel the presence of something staring out at her. Watching her.

Waiting.

"Stop!" I shout, as loud as I dare, and then I start hurrying after her.

With each step, the fear in my chest gets tighter and tighter, and I feel a sense of pure panic starting to fill my body. I've never felt like this before, but it's as if somehow the panic is being poured into me as I force my way through the overgrown cemetery, and after a moment I start trying to run. Thick brambles get in the way of my feet, causing me to stumble a couple of times, and there's a part of me that desperately wants to just turn around and go back to the safety of the wall. At the same time, I can't shake the feeling that Kerry's in danger, and I force myself to keep going faster and faster until, finally, I stumble out from the undergrowth and find myself on an uneven old stone path that seems to run around the perimeter of the church building.

I stop and listen, but at first I hear only the rustle of the wind in the grass.

A moment later I look over at one of the nearby windows. The church itself is mostly gray, but the window is jet-black and I realize after a few seconds that I'm getting colder and colder. I can't stop looking, however, and I feel as if I've been fixed in place by a gaze.

"Damn it!" Kerry says suddenly.

I turn, and at first I don't see her. Then, spotting what looks like an arched section around the church's side, I hurry over and find Kerry down on her knees in front of a large wooden door, fiddling with the lock.

"Let me guess," I say, seeing my own breath in the air as I speak, "you just happen to be an expert lock-picker, don't you?"

"I can get around," she replies, "but -"

Suddenly she gasps as her hands slip from the lock. To my surprise, I see that she's holding a knife.

"Did you steal that from the Neills' kitchen?" I ask.

"Oh, fuck off," she says, trying again with the knife. "No-one forced you to come out here. In fact, I didn't want you to come in the first place."

"Then why did you wake me up and ask me if I wanted to join you?"

"I told you, I felt sorry for you."

Rubbing my arms in an attempt to keep warm, I step closer and see that she's trying to slide the knife's blade into a slot between the doorway and the lock. Looking up for a moment, I can just about make out one edge of the spire rising high into the night sky, picked out by a line of moonlight. When I look back at Kerry, I can't help but notice that she looks so small as she remains on her knees in front of that huge wooden door.

"That's one big-ass lock," I point out. "Someone *really* didn't want anyone getting into this church." I peer closer. "It looks kinda modern, too, like someone updated it."

"Is there any chance you can actually be of practical help?" she asks, still struggling with the blade. "I don't need someone standing around, pointing out the obvious."

"You're never going to get that open," I tell her. "It looks like you'd need a bolt-cutter."

"Everything can be broken into," she replies, but then after a moment she sighs, gets to her feet and takes a step back. "You just have to be inventive."

"That door looks impregnable," I reply, as we stand and stare at the huge metal contraption that's been fixed in place. "No offense, but you'd have better luck trying to cut through the wood of the door itself."

"I know," she says, before suddenly turning and walking away, "but thanks for the insight, Einstein."

"So we're going home now, right?" I ask, following her, only to find that she's heading around to the next side of the building. "If there's another door, I'm sure it'll be just as secure."

"There isn't another door, I already checked."

She reaches down and picks up a rock from the ground, and then she takes off her jacket as she heads over to one of the windows.

"You can't do that!" I hiss, hurrying after her. "Are you insane?"

She puts her jacket against the window, which contains lots of little squares of glass held in place between part of some kind of metal lattice. Each pane is barely five or six inches wide.

"And what are you going to do after you've broken some glass?" I ask. "It's not like you can -"

Before I'm able to finish, she slams her elbow against part of the jacket, and I hear a dull thud.

"This is vandalism," I point out with a sigh. "If you get caught, they'll throw the book at you. I don't know much about you, Kerry, but I really don't think this is your first -"

She hits the jacket again, still trying to break the glass on the other side, but again the only sound is a faint thud that sounds pretty impotent.

"It's probably really thick," I add, "and, like, hundreds of years old. You're never going to -"

I flinch as she tries again, this time using her clenched right fist. Even *she* should be able to tell that she's wasting her time, and sure enough a moment later she steps back, drops the rock, and starts slipping back into her jacket. Then she steps forward and cups her hands around her eyes, trying to look through the glass and see into the church.

"Well?" I ask.

"Well what?"

"Well, do you see anything?"

"Yes."

"What?"

"I thought you didn't care?"

"What do you see, Kerry?"

"Why do you care?"

"I'm out here with you, aren't I?" I reply with a sigh.

"I'll tell you exactly what I see," she says, before taking another step back and turning to me. "Fuck all. It's way too dark in there. Loser."

"I guess it's not your night," I tell her, while rubbing my arms again for warmth. "Is there anything else you want to try before we go back to the cottage? Climb up the side of the building and try to get in through the bell-tower, maybe?"

She turns and looks up toward the spire.

THE HORROR OF BRIARWYCH CHURCH

"I was joking," I add, just in case she gets any bright ideas.

"I'm going to get into this place," she says, sounding absolutely determined. "Even if I have to nick some heavy machinery from somewhere, I'm getting inside. No-one has the right to keep Kerry Lawrence out of anywhere."

"Why do you even care?" I ask. "You don't strike me as the church-going type."

"You should have heard Caroline telling me to stay away from this place," she replies, "like I'm some kind of child. And that lock on the door, what's that all about? People don't want me going in, and that's enough of a reason. I want to see inside this place for myself, and I'm not letting anyone stop me."

Crouching down, she reaches into the undergrowth, and then she pulls out something that glints slightly in the moonlight.

"Cool," she says, standing and showing me a small silver crucifix. "I bet someone misses this. Do you reckon it's worth anything?"

She slips it into her pocket.

"No-one ever stops me doing anything," she adds. "Sometimes they try, but I always show them that they can't."

Turning, she stomps past me and heads back the way we came.

"So you're just trying to get into the church

to prove a point?" I call after her. "Isn't that kinda childish?"

I wait, before she disappears around the corner and I sigh as I realize that at least she seems to have given up for tonight. I look around, still feeling that sense of absolute dread, and then I glance at the window that Kerry tried to break. For a moment, staring at the glass squares, I once again get that feeling that somehow I'm being watched. I know that's nuts, of course, but the sensation grows until I force myself to turn and walk away, hurrying after Kerry. I just want to get back to the cottage, go to sleep, and wake up for that full English breakfast that Caroline promised would be ready at eight in the morning. Man, I'm so -

Stopping suddenly as I go around the corner, I see that Kerry's standing a little way ahead, staring at the church's big wooden door.

"Come on," I say as I head over to join her, "let's -"

And then I stop again, as I see that the wooden door is now wide open, revealing the pure pitch darkness of the church's interior.

CHAPTER FOUR
KERRY

"HEY, STOP!" MARK HISSES again as I step through the doorway and into the darkness. "You can't seriously be going in there!"

It's so cold in this church, colder even than it was outside. I'm wearing a jacket and I'm still almost shivering. Stopping for a moment, I stare straight ahead and squint slightly, but I swear I can't see anything at all. There's not even a hint of light. I've never been anywhere so completely dark before, and I feel as if I really, really shouldn't be here. It's as if the darkness is pushing back at me.

There's also a stale, fusty smell in the freezing damp air, and mixed in with that smell there's also a hint of something else, something I recognize. Burned petrol, maybe, or something similar.

I should leave. I don't know how I know that, but I do. I should not be here.

"Kerry, we have to go home now," Mark whines. "We're not allowed to be in here. This is a really bad idea."

Turning, I see his silhouette as he waits just outside the door. As much as I want to leave, there's no way I'm going to give him the satisfaction.

"So are you coming," I ask, "or are you an even bigger chicken than I thought?"

"Grow up," he replies. "How did you even open this thing, anyway?"

"It was open when I came back around."

"How did -"

"Obviously I did something when I was using the knife," I point out, in case his painfully slow brain can't quite figure things out. "I unlocked it without realizing, and then a gust of wind must have blown it open. Neat, huh? I've spent time on the streets, I know how to hustle."

"I don't like this," he replies.

"So I was right, you *are* a chicken."

"I'm not scared!" he says firmly, although I can hear the truth in his voice. He sounds cautious to say the least, and I'm pretty sure he's on the verge of pissing himself with fear. He's such a wimp. "I just don't see the point of being here! It's a dusty old church. What exactly are you expecting to find that's worth going in there?"

"Then wait outside or go back to the house," I reply, turning and stepping forward into the icy interior of the church. "I won't dob on you, I promise."

To be honest, it's way colder in here than I ever expected, and the darkness is really freaky. I'm not really sure that it's worth looking around, at least not at night, and I can still feel the icy darkness pushing against me. There's no way I'm going to back down, though, not after everything I just said to Mark. So I take a few more steps forward, and finally I spot a hint of moonlight against some large, high windows in the distance. I go over to take a closer look, only to bump straight into a stone wall.

Taking out my phone, I bring up the flashlight app and switch it on, and then I cast the beam around.

Spotting an open doorway, I head over and peer through. As I cast the flashlight's beam across the room, I realize that this looks like some kind of old office. I never knew that churches had offices, but I guess vicars need somewhere to get all their shit done. Making my way across the room, I see dust floating through the beam of light. I reckon no-one's been in here for a long time, and when I get to the desk I see that several sheets of old paper have been left scattered around, along with a couple that have been scrunched into balls and let in place.

I peer down at the papers, but the writing is totally faded. Maybe some old vicar used to sit here and write his boring sermons.

Next to the desk there's an old leather bag. I pick it up and set it on the desk, and then I start going through the various sections.

"What are you doing?" Mark asks from the doorway.

"Seeing if there's anything worth taking."

"You can't steal from a church."

"I don't think anyone's coming back for this shit," I point out, before turning the bag around and seeing that there's something engraved on a small gold buckle. "It's been abandoned."

I lean closer and squint as I try to read the words.

"Father L. Loveford," I whisper. "Huh. I wonder why Father L. Loveford didn't take his bag with him when he left? I guess he must've been in too much of a hurry. Still, cool name."

I take a look through the rest of the bag's pockets, only to find that they're empty, before hauling it over my shoulder and heading back toward the doorway.

"Outta my way, loser," I say to Mark, and then I intentionally bump against him as I head back out into the corridor. "Finders keepers."

"Kerry, I -"

"You're officially starting to bore me," I tell

him, and now I actually *am* starting to wish that he'd go away and leave me to explore this place alone. This church is way too cool for idiots like Mark to ruin. "You're just jealous that I'm the one who got us in here. Or is it the bag? Did you fancy a man-bag, Mark?"

Reaching an arched doorway, I aim my flashlight through to see what's next.

"Neat," I whisper, as I see the backs of wooden pews stretching way out before me. Most of them are badly damaged, as if they were attacked with something. After a moment, I realize that they actually look as if they were burned a long time ago. I guess maybe that's where part of the stench is coming from.

I'm in the main part of the church, whatever that's called. It's pretty big, with a high ceiling and huge stained-glass windows on either side. There's an aisle down the middle of the place, between the burned pews on either side, and at the far end there's a kind of raised platform section that I guess must be the altar. Churches are weird. I don't remember the last time I was in one; in fact, now I think about it, I don't even know that I *have* been in one. Maybe as a kid, if I was baptized and all that shit. Churchyards have always been fun places to get up to stuff at night, but churches themselves have never really caught my attention before tonight.

Still, as I wander along the aisle between the

burned pews, casting the light from my phone around, I've got to admit that this place is pretty cool. You could have a hell of a party in here.

"Kerry!"

Stopping, I aim the flashlight straight back at Mark. He's way behind me, in the archway that leads out into the entrance corridor, and I smile as he holds a hand up to shield his eyes. I try to aim the beam better, to really blind him.

"Come on," he continues, "this place is a dump. There's blatantly nothing here!"

"I know!" I call back to him, and I notice this time that my voice echoes slightly. "Cool!"

"But if -"

"Cool!" I yell, and sure enough my voice bounces around for a few seconds high above us. "Did you hear that?"

"Kerry -"

"Echo!" I shout.

"Echo!" my voice replies all around us. "Echo! Echo! Echo!"

"Fuck!" I shout.

"Fuck! Fuck! Fuck!"

"Not gonna join in?" I ask, turning to Mark again.

"I don't like it in here," he says, sounding more than a little stressed. "Can't you feel it?"

"Feel what?"

"It's in the air all around. Something's not

right here. It's like my skin's starting to crawl."

"If you don't want to be here," I reply, "then don't be. Jog on, and let me have my fun. You're just a pussy."

Turning, I head along the aisle until I reach the altar. I think the big stone table thing is the actual altar, so I haul myself up and sit on the edge. I set the old leather bag over my shoulder and I start swinging my legs, as I aim the flashlight down and see that there are some dusty old words carved into the altar's top section.

"What the fuck does that say?" I mutter, trying to pick out some of the words before giving up. I guess it's just some old nonsense that someone gave a shit about once. Maybe it's Latin.

"You shouldn't sit on that," Mark says from the distant archway.

"Are you still here?" I ask, looking over toward the far side of the altar. It's so cold in here now, my teeth are really starting to chatter. I swear it suddenly got much colder over the past few seconds.

"You're being disrespectful," Mark calls out.

"So? You're a pussy." I smile. "Pussy!"

My voice echoes.

"Pussy! Pussy! Pussy!"

"Stop!" Mark shouts, and his voice echoes too.

"Since when did you care?" I whisper,

rolling my eyes. I look at the letters for a moment longer, and then I turn and aim the flashlight at the area behind the altar. "I'm not -"

Suddenly I freeze as I see that there's a woman standing right behind me, wearing a black dress and staring straight at me with angry eyes.

Before I can pull away, she reaches out and grabs the side of my face. Her hand is icy and her grip is firm, and when I try to cry out I feel as if my jaw is frozen. All I can manage is a very faint, gasping whimper as the woman slowly leans closer to me.

The entire left side of my face is so cold now, and the pain is intense, as the woman slowly turns my head until I'm looking back along the aisle. At the same time, my trembling hands drop the phone onto the top of the altar. The beam is blasting back toward the burned pews, and I can just about see Mark over in the archway.

"Please," I try to whisper, as tears run down my cheeks and the pain intensifies, "help me. Please help me, please..."

The woman leans over my shoulder, staring directly into my eyes.

"What are you doing here?" she asks, her voice filled with hatred. "What do you want in my church?"

CHAPTER FIVE
MARK

"WHAT DID YOU SAY?" I ask, sighing as I try to hear Kerry. "Why don't you come over here and we can leave, okay? This place is really giving me the creeps."

I wait, but she's still sitting there on the altar. A moment ago she tossed her phone down, and now the light is shining out across the damaged pews. I can barely see Kerry at all, but she seems to be sitting bolt upright and she hasn't yelled at me for a couple of minutes now, which is something of a record. I think she's talking, though. I can hear some kind of whisper coming from over there, but I can't make out any of the words. Typical. This is the moment she chooses to stop being loud.

"Okay, I'm out of here," I say, turning to

leave. At the last moment, however, I stop and look back at her. I was hoping to call her bluff, but she's still up there on the altar.

No matter how much I want to get out of here, it wouldn't be right to just leave her here. She might be a pain in the ass, but I'd feel bad if she ended up getting hypothermia, so finally I sigh as I start making my way toward her along the aisle. As I walk, I have to hold a hand up in front of my eyes, to protect myself from the beam of that flashlight. I swear, I'm so mad at her right now, I'm going to really have to hold back so that I don't call her all the bad names under the sun.

I can definitely hear her talking up ahead, but she's kind of whispering and I can't quite make out the words. Maybe this is part of some stupid game.

"Okay, fine," I say finally as I get to the far end of the aisle and lower my hand. The light isn't so dazzling now. "What gives? What do you want?"

I wait, but she's just sitting there all alone on the altar with a really strange expression on her face, almost like she's terrified. She has her head tilted to the right and she's staring at me, and after a moment I realize that there seem to be tears running down her cheeks.

"What the hell?" I whisper, stepping closer and noticing that it's much colder here, colder even than the aisle. "Kerry, what's got into you?"

"Why are you here?" she gasps, her voice shaking so badly that I can barely even make out what she's saying. "What are you doing here in my church?"

"What am I doing here?" I reply. "In *your* church?"

I wait for her to follow up with some lame joke, but after a moment I realize that her whole body seems to be trembling violently.

"I don't *know* why I'm here," I tell her, starting to feel majorly exasperated that she's keeping us here. "I guess I just didn't want you to go wandering around in the dark all by yourself. I guess maybe, just maybe, I'm a gentleman. Did you consider that? Maybe I'm not a complete asshole who runs off and abandons people. But you have to come with me now, yeah? We're getting out of this stupid church."

Again I wait, and again she simply stares at me.

Her bottom lip is wobbling and more tears are rolling down her cheeks. I've got to admit, she's doing a really good job of acting like she's scared. Maybe she could be an actor one day.

"Why did you come?" she stammers finally. "You... You have no right to be here."

"No right to be here?" I raise a skeptical eyebrow. "That's rich, coming from the one who broke the lock. Now let's go!"

"You should not have tried to enter this place," she continues, tilting her head a little more and letting out a faint gasp that sounds almost painful. "This... This church is not... for you."

"Huh?"

I wait, but now she just seems to have gone bat-shit crazy.

"We're done here, okay?" I say finally, stepping closer to her and reaching out to grab her and pull her off the altar. "I've had more than enough of your rubbish and I'm freezing to death and -"

As soon as I touch her icy hand, she cries out and falls forward, landing against me. Startled, I fumble to keep her from falling all the way off the altar, but then she slithers down and her knees buckle. All I can do is keep hold of the sides of her arms and lower her down, and I'm actually starting to think that she's fainted or something like that. Unless this really *is* just one of her stupid jokes and she's taking it way too far.

"Hey, are you alright?" I ask, crouching next to her as she slumps back against the front of the altar. "What the hell were you just on about there?"

She turns to me, with that same horrified look in her eyes, and for a moment she seems frozen in place.

"Okay, you win," I continue. "You've

freaked me out. Well done. Now can we please get out of here?"

"She..."

I wait, but her voice trails off.

"What?" I ask. "Come on, this is boring."

"Did you...."

Again I wait.

"Did I what?" I say with a sigh. "Can you just get on with it, so we can leave?"

"But she..."

She pauses, and then slowly she looks up toward the edge of the altar above us. For a moment, her eyes seem genuinely filled with fear.

"She..."

Suddenly she scrambles to her feet and backs away until she bumps against one of the pews. She's not looking at me, however; instead, she seems to be staring straight at the altar.

"Kerry?" I continue, still kneeling on the hard floor. "What -"

"Didn't you see her?" she gasps. "Tell me you saw her! You must have seen her!"

"What's that smell?" I ask, sniffing the air and then noticing some kind of liquid dribbling down from the top of the altar. There's more on the ground too, with little drops and sprinkles running all the way over to where Kerry's standing. "Dude," I say cautiously, "please tell me you didn't just pee your pants."

"She was right there!" she says, pointing at the altar. She's still crying. "You saw her! You must have seen her!"

"I didn't see anything except *you*, acting the fool," I reply, getting to my feet and then turning to look at the altar. Picking up Kerry's phone, I shine the beam of light around, but all I see is stone walls. "I'm really not in the mood for one of your lame practical jokes. And if you think you're gonna scare me, you should just save yourself the effort."

"Didn't you *hear* her?" Kerry asks.

Turning, I see that she's touching the left side of her face, as if she's in pain.

"Hear who?" I reply.

"She was talking to you! First she was talking to me, then when you came up here she started talking to you too!"

"What?" I ask with a scowl. "There was nobody talking to me except you, and you were being really weird."

"She asked why we were here," she stammers.

"Huh?" I step toward her, carefully avoiding the patches of what I'm pretty sure is pee. "*You* were talking to me, Kerry," I remind her. "You were asking me all these stupid-ass questions and telling me that I've got no right to be in this church."

"No, *she* was saying that," she sobs. "She

was holding my head. She was right next to me and she was talking to both of us!"

"What?"

I wait for her to burst out laughing, but she really seems to be taking this prank too far. I'll give her credit for her commitment, but she needs to learn when enough's enough.

"Okay," I say with a heavy sigh, "you know what? I'm officially too cold and tired for this -"

Suddenly she turns and runs, racing back along the aisle with the leather bag over her shoulder, and then finally she disappears out into the corridor. I can hear her footsteps until she gets outside, and then for a moment I hear the sound of her running at full whack through the overgrown cemetery.

"*Excuse* me?" I ask out loud, shocked that she suddenly took off like that. "Seriously? I follow you into this creepy-ass church and I wait around for you in the freezing cold, and then *you* just take off on *me*?"

I wait, but she's long gone and I can't help but think that she's taking this so-called joke and really running with it. Looking down at the patch of liquid on the altar, I lean a little closer, to prove to myself that it's just water, but then I recoil as I realize that it's actually, genuinely pee. Either this girl is completely crazy, crazier than I ever imagined, or she just literally peed herself in order to go all-in with a joke.

"Gross," I mutter.

For a moment, I cast the phone's flashlight beam around, but of course there's no sign of anyone else here. All I see are the church's stone walls, although after a few seconds I notice that there are some dark patches in some areas, as if there was once some kind of fire here. I guess that'd line up with the damage to the pews, which look like they were on fire at some point. In fact, I'm starting to really get the feeling that some weird shit once went down in this church, which maybe explains why I feel so uneasy right now. This place isn't exactly very welcoming.

"Screw this," I say finally, before turning and making my way back along the aisle. "I am so out of here."

***

Taking great care to not make any noise, I very gently shut the back door and then I wait for a moment. The cottage is dark and silent, and there's no sign that anyone is awake, so I reach down and slowly turn the key before heading across the kitchen and into the hallway.

At least this place is warm. We must have been out for about an hour, which means it's a little after 3am. Climbing the stairs, I try to avoid making any sounds, although a couple of the steps creak beneath my feet. By the time I get to the landing, however, there's still no hint of movement coming from Mr. and Mrs. Neill's bedroom, so I guess they must have actually slept through everything.

I step toward my room, before stopping as I realize I can hear Kerry sobbing nearby.

I hesitate, telling myself that this is all a stupid game and that I shouldn't encourage her, but those sobs sound so real and finally I head over to her door. I listen to her sobs for a moment longer and then I gently tap on the door. She doesn't respond, but I really want to check that she's okay so I gently turn the handle and push the door open, only to find that the room is dark.

Peering through, I see that Kerry is sitting on her bed with her arms around her knees. She's crying like I've never seen anyone cry before, and tears are absolutely streaming down her face.

"Hey," I whisper, before stepping into the room and then carefully shutting the door. "I just came to see if you're alright."

As I head over to the bed and then, I bump my feet against something on the floor. Looking down, I see the leather bag, so I pick it up and set it on the table. Then, figuring that I might as well stay for a few minutes, I sit on the edge of the bed and wait for Kerry to say something. She's looking at me, but she seems absolutely horrified. If she's acting, she's damn good at it. Maybe she really *is* crazy? Like *properly* crazy.

"Got your phone," I say, holding it up to show her.

She doesn't say anything, so I reach over and set it on the little stand next to her bed. Spotting her charging cable, I plug it in for her as well.

"So what was that all about, huh?" I ask, keeping my voice low as I turn to her again. "You really freaked me out back there. Respect where it's due, you went all in."

Again I wait, and again she simply continues to weep while staring at me. She's shaking, too, which seems odd given that this whole cottage is nice and warm.

"I get it," I continue, "you like playing games, but I can I please ask you to -"

"Did you really not see anything?" she whimpers suddenly, interrupting me.

"Like what?"

"Just tell me what you saw."

"I didn't see anything!"

"You must have done!"

"Can you give me an idea what I'm supposed to have seen?" I ask.

"She was right there!" she snaps.

"Keep your voice down," I reply. I reach out and touch her arm, but she immediately pulls away as if she thinks I'm about to attack her. "Sorry," I

THE HORROR OF BRIARWYCH CHURCH

add, "I just... I swear, I didn't see anyone else in that church. You were talking and being weird, and then you kind of slumped down off the altar and landed on the floor. Then you bolted and left me there."

"I didn't talk!" she says. "I *couldn't* talk!"

Sighing, I look over at the window as I try to get my thoughts together. Back in the church, I was sure this was all an act, but now I'm genuinely worried she might be sick in the head. I don't actually know her that well, but it never occurred to me until this moment that maybe she's got some kind of serious mental issue. Maybe she's unstable or something, or she's a fantasist. For the first time, I'm actually starting to feel sorry for her.

"Never mind," she says suddenly, and I turn to see that she's wiping tears from her eyes. "You don't believe me. No-one ever believes me about anything. You're just like all the rest."

"I'm just saying, I -"

"Can you get out of my room now, please?"

"Kerry -"

"Can you get out?" she continues, starting to sound annoyed now. "Or do I have to scream and tell Mr. and Mrs. Neill that you came in and started being weird to me. They'll believe me, you know. I'll tell them you tried to -"

"Forget it," I say, getting to my feet and heading to the door, where I stop and turn to look back at her. "You've got problems, do you know that? Like, serious problems."

"I don't want to talk about it."

"If you really saw something in the church, then you need -"

"I said, I don't want to talk about it! Can you shut the door as you leave, please?"

"But if -"

"Can you get out of my room, please, Mark?" she suddenly calls out loudly, clearly intending for Mr. and Mrs. Neill to hear. "Why are you sneaking in here in the middle of the night, anyway?"

Realizing that she's never going to talk seriously, I step out onto the landing and pull the door gently shut. As I do so, however, I spot movement nearby, and I turn to see that Caroline Neill is watching me from the door that leads into the master bedroom.

I open my mouth to apologize, but I know I've been caught red-handed.

"Do I need to worry about anything?" she asks.

I can hear her husband snoring in the darkness of the room.

After a moment, I shake my head.

"You should get back to bed now," she continues. "Breakfast's at eight."

I nod.

"Well go on, then," she says. "No more

creeping about at night, please. You weren't going to go outside, were you?"

"No," I reply, although in that moment I realize that we left the church door open, which means someone'll know people went inside. They'd be crazy not to suspect it was us. "Actually, we -"

"Go to bed, Mark," she says, cutting me off. "We can talk in the morning."

I nod, before heading to my room. Caroline is still watching me as I gently bump the door shut, and then I wait for a few seconds until I hear her door closing. I so badly want to go back through to Kerry and ask what's wrong with her, but I'm starting to think that she must have a major screw loose. I think maybe she really believes she saw a woman in the church tonight.

CHAPTER SIX
KERRY

I SCREAM AS SHE tilts my head back, and I feel her ice-cold fingers pressing against my throat as she leans closer to my face.

"What do you want here?" she snarls.

Too terrified to reply, I simply continue to shiver as I stare up into her sunken dead eyes. She's so pale, and the skin is clinging to the bones of her face. She looks like someone who just climbed out of a coffin.

"Answer me!" she hisses, leaning even closer. "What are you doing in my church?"

"Please," I stammer, barely managing to get the words out, "leave me alone. I don't want to -"

Suddenly she screams.

Gasping, I suddenly sit up in bed and clutch

my throat. For a few seconds, I can still feel those icy fingers, as if they somehow pierced my skin and slid deep into my neck. The sensation slowly fades, however, as I realize I must have just fallen asleep and had a bad dream. There's light outside now, beyond the closed curtains, and after a moment I hear voices talking outside as some people walk past the cottage.

Checking my phone, I see that it's almost exactly 8am. A moment later, I realize I can smell eggs and bacon. And then, as I climb out of bed so I can go and have a shower, I spot that old leather bag on the table.

***

"Just in time for a fry-up!" Caroline says with a smile as I stop in the kitchen doorway. "I was going to come up and knock for you, Kerry, but then I heard you in the shower. Do you want the works? Egg, bacon, sausages, beans, hash browns, tomato and mushroom?"

I stare at the food that's cooking in various pots and pans. For a moment, I feel absolutely starving, but then suddenly something lurches in the pit of my stomach and I have to look away. The thought of food makes me feel like I'm going to vomit.

"We have other things if you're not a full

English kind of girl," Caroline continues, as I take deep breaths in an attempt to calm my stomach. "Help yourself to anything that's in the fridge. The cheese is from a local cheese-maker who lives just around the corner, and the jam and marmalade is all home-made."

"Great," I mutter, although once again the thought of food makes me feel pretty weird.

Heading over to the sink, I pour myself a glass of water. I can tell out the corner of my eye that Mark is watching me, and the last thing I want is to let him see that I feel weird. I swear, if he asks me one more time whether I'm okay, I'm gonna -

"Are you okay?"

I flinch, but I somehow manage to keep from turning and glaring at him.

"I'm fine," I reply through gritted teeth, before taking a drink. I thought some water would make me feel better, but instead the sensation of water running down into my stomach almost makes me retch. A moment later the sound of frying food seems to get louder, and I have to really focus to keep from heaving all over the sink.

"I thought we could take a little walk around the village after breakfast," Caroline continues. "I know that probably sounds pretty boring to you two city-dwellers, but I can show you where a few things are. Then I can maybe treat us all to some sandwiches at the pub."

"That'd be nice," Mark says. "Thank you."

Why is he so polite all the time? Why doesn't he -

Suddenly I feel a lurching sensation in my belly, as if I'm about to vomit. I grip the side of the sink, but fortunately the feeling passes pretty quickly. Something's definitely not right, though, and I'm starting to feel this weird sense of weakness that doesn't make any sense. At the same time, the sensation's strangely familiar, and there's some kind of dizziness creeping in as well. I guess I just need to get my head together and ignore that weird-ass dream I had last night, but -

Suddenly an icy hand touches my arm.

"What were you doing in my church?"

Startled, I turn and see a figure standing right next to me. I have to blink a couple of times before I'm able to properly see the figure's face, and I realize that it's Caroline. Her hand still feels ice-cold, and after a moment I pull away from her grip.

"Kerry?" she says cautiously. "Are you okay? You're looking a little peaky."

"I'm fine."

"Your color's off. You look pale."

"I told you, I'm fine."

"How's your temperature?"

She reaches up to touch my forehead with the back of her hand, but I pull away.

"Please stop fussing," I say, trying to smile

so that she can see I'm fine. "I'm always like this in the mornings. I'm a really slow-riser. I can't even remember the last time I was up before midday."

I glance at Mark and see that he's staring at me with that same gormless expression that he's always got.

"Haven't you got anything better to do?" I ask. "You're being weird again."

He looks back down at his cup of tea.

"Don't push yourself too hard, okay?" Caroline says as she heads back over to the cooker and starts dishing up breakfast. "Don't underestimate the stresses involved with a big move. I know Briarwych must seem like a sleepy little place, but it's going to be a real culture shock for you guys. You'll get used to it eventually, but in the meantime -"

"Why would I get used to it?" I ask. "I'm only staying for a month."

"Well, that's the initial trial period but -"

"A month and that's it," I add. "I don't do countryside and rural. As soon as I hit sixteen, I'm going off on my own and people like Maxine Trevor can kiss my ass."

"That's your choice," Caroline says, carefully setting some fried eggs onto the plates. "Maybe you'll change your mind."

"Yeah, I don't think I -"

Suddenly I feel a twisting pain low down in

my belly, and I actually almost gag a little. Leaning back against the counter, I realize there are pinpricks of cold sweat spreading across my forehead, and my throat feels very dry as I swallow. For a moment I can't remember when I felt like this before, but then I think back to last night in the church. Is that when I felt it? When that woman touched my face and started asking all those questions? I tried to tell myself this morning that she wasn't real, that I was just tripping out on cow-shit-filled country air, but I swear that bitch's face is burned into my retinas.

I can almost see her right now, everywhere I look.

"Kerry?"

Turning, I see that Mark's staring at me again.

"You look white as a sheet," he adds.

"Go fuck yourself."

"Language, please," Caroline says, glancing at me. "Sorry, but this is a no-swearing household."

"Go screw yourself, then," I tell Mark.

"And let's try to keep it civil," Caroline adds.

"He started it."

At the same time, I reach back and grip the side of the counter. My knees are trembling now and I'm worried I might collapse. I just need to get some strength back and go back upstairs, and wait things out in my room. I can stay in there all morning and pretend I'm just being a moody little bitch. The problem, though, is that right now I'm not sure I'd make it all the way over to the bottom of the stairs, let alone up to the landing and then into my room. If I faint, I'm going to end up looking like a total asshole. Everyone would laugh at me forever.

"Will you *stop* staring at me?" I snap at Mark.

"Sorry," he mutters, looking away as Caroline sets a plate down in front of him.

She's looking at me, too. I can tell she's worried.

I turn away, but I can feel them still looking at me. They're both staring, and it's as if their gazes are drilling into the side of my face, burning through my flesh. I try to ignore them both, but finally I feel like I have to say something, so I turn to them.

"Can you both just -"

I freeze as I see that they're not looking at me. Caroline is at the cooker, and Mark's reading something on his phone. I swear I felt them staring, but I guess maybe I'm just getting a little jumpy. The countryside's really getting to me.

"I think I'm just going to go up to my room," I tell Caroline, as my head starts to feel really heavy. I can barely even keep it from drooping, and I think I'm starting to properly sweat. "I want to be alone for a while. I might go back to sleep for a few hours."

"That's okay," she replies, turning to me before tilting her head slightly. "You shouldn't have come into my church."

"What?" I stammer, and now as I stare at her I swear I can't actually see her face. Like, I know she *has* a face, I'm looking right at it, but somehow I can't get my eyes to see the details.

And that voice didn't sound like her at all.

"You intruded," the voice says after a moment. I'm staring at Caroline, but I can't tell whether or not her mouth is moving. "You desecrated my church. For that, you must pay."

I try to ask what she means, but I don't quite want to give away the fact that I'm feeling weird. At the same time, I'm getting weaker and weaker, as if all the strength is just draining out of my body. And then, suddenly, I realize where I've felt this feeling before.

In the alley, when I was dying.

This is exactly how I felt that night. The doctors said I was so close to death, that it was a miracle the ambulance got to me in time, that another minute would have been too long. I felt exactly like this, and now I can feel a sense of panic rising through my chest as I look around the kitchen. I can see and not see at the same time.

There are shapes, but I can't quite make them turn into actual things that I recognize. I can just about tell that Mark's still at the table, and that Caroline's over by the cooker, or is that Caroline in the doorway? Wait, there's someone else here, a figure wearing dark clothes standing in the doorway and staring at me. I turn to her, but I can't properly see her.

I want this feeling to go away right now. This is exactly how it was, just before the ambulance crew got to me, when I was seconds from dying.

"Um," I manage to say finally, as I start shivering violently, "I think I..."

I pause, and then suddenly everything goes black and I feel myself slump down to the floor.

AMY CROSS

CHAPTER SEVEN
MARK

"KERRY!"

Racing from the chair, I drop to my knees just a few seconds too late to catch her. She drops like a stone, banging her head against the side of the counter and then flopping onto her side like some kind of rag doll.

"Kerry!" I shout again, reaching out and touching the side of her face, and finding that her skin is like ice. "What happened? Are you okay?"

"Get out of the way," Caroline says, kneeling next to me and pushing my shoulder. "Mark, I'm trained for this kind of thing. Just give us some space."

"Is she okay?" I ask.

Instead of replying, Caroline reaches down

79

and gently nudges Kerry's arm.

"Kerry?" she says cautiously. "Can you hear me?"

"Why's she sweating so much?" I ask. "She looked really sick from the moment she came down this morning. I could tell something was wrong with her!"

Caroline leans over her and presses two fingers against the side of her neck. She must be searching for a pulse. After a moment, she mutters something under her breath and grabs Kerry's left wrist, where she checks again. As I wait for her to say that Kerry's okay, each second seems to last an eternity.

"Is her heart beating?" I stammer finally. "Tell me she's going to be okay!"

I wait, but she's too busy checking Kerry's other wrist, and I can tell from the look on her face that something's seriously wrong. It's almost as if she can't find a pulse at all.

"Call an ambulance," she says suddenly, as she leans over Kerry's body and prepares to do some chest compressions. "Mark, call an ambulance right now!"

Struggling to my feet, I hurry over to the table, only to realize that my phone's upstairs. I turn to look for another, just as Caroline starts performing the compressions on Kerry and counting loudly. I'm about to ask her where I can find the nearest phone, but then I remember seeing a landline in the next room so I race through and pick it up, and then I freeze for a moment before remembering the right number. I jab 999 and then I wait for someone to answer on the other end of the line. Again, everything seems to be happening so slowly.

There's a brief ringing tone, and then a burst of static forces me to pull the phone away from my ear.

"Hello?" I shout, unsure as to whether anyone has answered. "Are you there?"

The static returns, flaring loudly. I guess it's possible that there's a human voice lost in the mix somewhere, in which case there's at least a chance they can hear me even if I can't hear them.

"I need an ambulance!" I explain. "I don't even know the address, but we're in Briarwych, near the church! We're in the little cottage with roses outside. Please, she's really sick, she collapsed and I don't think she's breathing! Can you get someone here really fast?"

I wait, with tears in my eyes, but all I hear is another burst of loud, distorted static.

"Hello?" I shout, before cutting the call and then dialing again.

I wait, but the static returns and – if anything – it's louder than ever.

"If anyone can hear me," I continue

desperately, "trace this call and send an ambulance. We're in Briarwych and she's unconscious. I don't think she's breathing, we need help!" I wait, hoping that I might hear someone reply even deep in the wall of static. "I'm going to try a mobile!" I add finally, before putting the phone down.

Trying to stay calm, I look around for a moment before hurrying back to the kitchen. My mind is racing, but all I know is that Kerry needs me to get this right.

"Where's your phone?" I shout. "I don't even know who to -"

Stopping suddenly, I see that Caroline is no longer performing the compressions on Kerry. Instead she's simply sitting on the floor, staring down at Kerry's lifeless body.

"What is it?" I ask, my heart racing as I wait to be told that everything's okay. "Why aren't you doing anything?"

She pauses, before turning to me with tear-filled eyes.

"Why aren't you doing anything?" I shout. "Help her!"

***

"The autopsy will tell us exactly what happened," Doctor Groves says calmly, as we sit in the living room, "but for now it's difficult for me to suggest a cause of death. From what you described, it's possible that something happened in her heart. Equally, the cause of death might have been an aneurysm, something in the brain. I'd really prefer not to speculate."

"But are you sure she's dead?" I ask, as more tears roll down my cheeks. "What if she's just in a coma?"

"I'm very sorry," he replies, "but I'm afraid the time of death has already been established."

"But you might be wrong!"

"I'm sorry."

"Can't you check again?" I plead. "Just in case you missed something? What if..."

My voice trails off as I try to think of something, anything, that might help. A moment later, hearing a bumping sound, I turn just in time to see that the two paramedics from the ambulance have finished loading Kerry's body onto the stretcher. Doctor Groves had to call them after he came from his house down the road; my phone calls apparently didn't get through. The paramedics are strapping Kerry down now, and they've already put her into a body bag. She can't be dead, though. I mean, half an hour ago she was alive, she was telling me to fuck off.

She can't be gone, not so quickly.

"I knew she looked ill," Caroline says after a moment. "As soon as she came downstairs, I could tell that something wasn't right." She turns to me. "You saw it too, didn't you? She looked pale, like she was sick."

I nod.

"What about last night?" Doctor Groves asks. "How did she seem?"

"Fine," Caroline tells him, before turning to me again. "Did she say anything to you?"

I shake my head.

"Sometimes these things can come on very suddenly," the doctor continues. "It's quite possible that whatever happened was something that began to develop during the night. We really will have to wait until the autopsy's complete before we know for sure. I'll get it hurried through at the hospital in Crenford, so hopefully we can have some answers in the next day or two, and I'll come and speak to you about those results as soon as I get them. It might be that -"

"We went to the church last night," I blurt out suddenly.

They both stare at me, as if they're not quite sure that they heard me correctly.

"We went to the church," I continue, sniffing back more tears as I turn to Caroline. "I'm so sorry, but we snuck out some time after midnight. It wasn't my idea, I swear, I only went because I wanted to make sure she was okay. I'm sorry I lied when I saw you in the middle of the night, but... I mean, it can't be anything to do with that, can it?"

"What exactly were you doing in the cemetery?" Caroline asks cautiously.

"We weren't in the cemetery," I tell her, and now my voice is trembling slightly. "Not really. We were in the actual church."

"That's impossible," Doctor Groves says. "The church is locked. It's been locked for a long time."

"She got the door open somehow."

"Impossible."

"She did!"

"But -"

He pauses, before turning to Caroline. They both look really worried.

"You went *inside*?" Caroline asks finally.

"Only for a few minutes," I reply. "Ten, maybe, but no more than that. She started acting weird while we were in there. It was almost like she was hallucinating or something."

Caroline turns to Doctor Groves, and I can tell now that they're both worried.

"She didn't hit her head or anything!" I continue. "Not that I saw, anyway. She just started saying weird things, and then she ran home. Please, I know we shouldn't have done it, I know it's bad, but nothing happened! At least, nothing that could have caused this. It's just a coincidence!" I turn to

Doctor Groves. "Isn't it?"

"Well, the..."

His voice trails off, and for a few seconds he seems genuinely troubled by something.

"If nothing happened, then nothing happened," Caroline says finally, but it sounds as if she's trying to convince herself. "And that's what you're saying, Mark, isn't it? That nothing happened?" She stares at me intently. "Nothing happened in the church, did it?"

"No," I reply.

She sighs, as if she's relieved.

"I mean," I continue, "she got a bit weird. She was sitting on the altar. I told her not to, but she went up there anyway and for a few minutes she was saying all this weird stuff, and then she said she'd seen a woman. But there wasn't a woman, I swear. So maybe she was sick already, and she was seeing things. That makes sense, doesn't it?"

I wait, but nobody says anything.

"Going to the church last night can't be what made this happen," I add, even though I can feel a sense of dread starting to creep up through my chest and onto my shoulders, pushing me down into the sofa. "Nothing bad happened at the church! I swear!"

Again I wait, but a moment later I hear the front door opening.

"What happened?" Brian asks, hurrying

through from the hallway. "Caroline, what's wrong? I saw your missed calls. Why's there an ambulance outside?"

Before anyone can say anything, the paramedics start wheeling the stretcher through, taking Kerry's dead body out to the ambulance. I want to stop them, to ask them to check one last time that there hasn't been some kind of mistake, but deep down I know there's no point. Kerry's dead.

CHAPTER EIGHT
MARK

GASPING FOR BREATH, I finally reach the top of the hill and stop to lean against the cemetery wall. I ran all the way here from the cottage, after suddenly feeling as if I was going to go crazy in there. Caroline and Doctor Groves were going over everything again, and I swear my head was about to burst.

In fact, I still feel that way.

Spotting an old, rickety wooden noticeboard, I head over and see faded pieces of paper still pinned inside. There are a few old notices about sermons and events in the church, but it looks like nothing new has been put on this board for years. And then, as my anger feels like it's about to explode, I kick one of the noticeboard's wooden legs. The entire structure shudders, so I kick it again, then again and again as I let my anger take over. For a moment all I feel is pure, blind fury, and I don't stop kicking until suddenly the wooden post gives way and breaks, and the noticeboard starts falling down. At the last second, the other post holds strong, but – as I step back to look at the damage I caused – I see that it's tilting at a forty-five degree angle.

Sighing, I step around the noticeboard and try to fix the damage I caused. I'm still angry, but I know I shouldn't have lashed out. The wooden leg is properly broken, but I manage to prop it back into place so that at least the noticeboard looks straight again. I hate these little bursts of anger that I get. They're so stupid, and they don't actually achieve anything.

Stepping back, I see that the noticeboard looks pretty good now.

Taking a deep breath, I look over toward the church, and I'm surprised to see that there's a man kneeling in front of the wooden door, working on the lock. I watch him for a moment, and then I head over to the gate. There's a part of me that just wants to turn and run, to get as far as possible from this place, but at the same time I want to know what happened here. Plus, in the daylight the church doesn't look quite so creepy. After opening the gate I push my way through the overgrown grass and weeds, and finally I reach the bare patch in front of the church's door.

The man glances at me for a moment, before returning his attention to the new lock that he's installing.

"You must be one of the new faces I heard about," he mutters, sounding distinctly unimpressed. "I don't suppose you know anything about this door mysteriously getting opened in the night, do you?"

"I'm sorry," I tell him.

He mutters something under his breath as he gets back to work.

"What is this place?" I ask.

He turns to me again.

"Why do people talk about it like they're scared of it?" I continue.

"I'm not sure I -"

"I just saw their faces right now," I tell him. "As soon as I mentioned this church, Mrs. Neill and Doctor Groves looked horrified. It's like just mentioning the place made them scared. Why?"

He stares at me for a moment.

"Just leave it alone," he says finally. "Don't ask questions when you can already tell that people don't want to answer them."

"But why's it locked in the first place?" I reply. "It's a church. Aren't churches supposed to be open, for people go and pray?"

"No-one's prayed in this church for a very long time."

"Why not?"

"You didn't actually go inside last night, did you?"

"The door was open! I mean, it was locked, but then it opened."

"Don't be so stupid, of course it didn't."

"I swear, she used a knife to -"

"This was one of the most advanced locks on the market," he says angrily, interrupting me. "Believe me, I'm the one who researched it and installed it, so I know. I tested it, too. Every few years I change this thing for something newer and more sturdy, so there's simply no way that a pair of kids with a knife could have got it to open."

"Then how did it open?" I ask.

He hesitates, but I guess he doesn't have an answer for that. I stare at him for a moment, before looking at the new lock that he's still in the process of fixing onto the door. It looks even sturdier than the one Kerry managed to break last night.

"Why are you doing this?" I ask finally. "Why do you have all this security, just to keep a church door shut?"

"You don't know anything, and I'd advise you to keep it that way." He turns back to the lock and resumes his work, screwing one of the metal plates into place. "You might be living here for now, but this church has nothing to do with you. It was here before you were born, and it'll be here long after all of us are gone. And the door will remain locked."

"She's dead," I tell him.

He turns to me again.

"My friend died this morning," I continue, and I can once again feel tears in my eyes. "Or whatever she was. Yeah, okay, we came here last night, and somehow we got through this door. We spent all of about ten minutes inside this church, and my friend started acting really strange. Less than half a day later, she's dead in a bag in the back of an ambulance. She collapsed this morning during breakfast. But that wasn't anything to do with this church, was it? I mean, she was talking about seeing someone inside, but that was just because she was sick. The fact that we came into this church is just a coincidence, isn't it?"

I wait, but he's got a weird look on his face. It's like the expression I saw on Caroline and Doctor Grover earlier.

"I'm sorry about your friend," he says finally, "but whatever happened to her, it sounds like it was just bad luck. Now if you don't mind, I really need to fix this lock. We can't leave the place open. After all, you never know when some idiot kids might break in and cause damage."

He turns and starts screwing another section

into place.

"Oh," he adds, "and don't take this the wrong way, but maybe Briarwych isn't for the likes of you. Maybe you should think about moving on. You've already caused more than enough trouble."

***

"Fucking countryside assholes!" I mutter under my breath as I push the last of my clothes back into my backpack. "Why the hell would anyone want to live in a place like this, anyway?"

"Knock knock."

Startled, I turn to see Maxine Trevor standing in the doorway.

"Hey," she says, with tears in her eyes, "I came as soon as I heard. Do you mind if I come in for a moment?"

"I'm all packed," I tell her. "Can we just talk in the car?"

"In the car?" She steps into the room. "Why are you packing, Mark?"

"I can't stay here now, can I?" I point out. "I mean, I've been here less than twenty-four hours and Kerry's already dead. There's no way I can stick around. This place is cursed or something."

I wait for her to agree with me, but she's just staring at me as if she's surprised by the fact that I want to leave.

"Sit down, Mark," she says finally.

"But -"

"Please." She gestures toward the bed. "You must be so shocked and upset. Mrs. Neill told me that you were in the room when Kerry collapsed."

I hesitate for a moment, before heading over and sitting down. I put my head in my hands as she sits next to me, and I take a deep breath as I realize that I don't know what to say. I just want to punch something. Maybe I should go and take another crack at that noticeboard. Then again, last time I just ended up feeling silly. Looking down at my hands, I try to imagine the anger draining out through my fingertips.

"I didn't know you or Kerry for very long," Mrs. Trevor says after a moment. "The funny thing with Kerry is that she was always so antagonistic, like she was trying to take on the whole world. By the time her file reached my desk, she had a string of referrals as long as any I've ever seen, and plenty of police reports as well. I don't know how much she told you about herself, but a while back she was very badly hurt in a stabbing. I read the medical notes, and it's a miracle that she survived. I guess that whole incident must have left its mark, because she seemed convinced that everyone was out to get her." She takes a deep breath, and there are still tears in her eyes. "I liked her, though. I admired her refusal to do everything she was told, even if she drove me crazy sometimes."

"We snuck out last night," I tell her.

"I know."

"We went to the church."

"I know."

"We didn't break in, though! The door just came open!"

She sighs.

"That part is a little difficult to believe," she says.

"It's true! I saw it!"

"Well, maybe. I don't suppose it matters right now."

"And she started acting weird in there."

"Mrs. Neill told me that you mentioned that."

"Could that have anything to do with what happened this morning?"

"It's possible," she explains. "Maybe she was already feeling a little off last night, but she didn't think it was anything serious."

"And could that have made her hallucinate?"

"I'm not a doctor, Mark," she replies, "but hallucinations might well be a sign that something wasn't right in her head."

"There's nothing wrong with that place, is there?" I ask.

"What do you mean?"

"People act all weird whenever that church is mentioned," I tell her. "I don't know what shit they think they've got going on here, but all we did was go into the church and look around. Kerry started acting weirdly, she seemed to be hallucinating, but going into the church didn't make her sick, did it? I mean, it couldn't have." I wait for her to answer. "Could it?"

"Of course not," she says finally. "You don't think I just randomly plopped the pair of you down here, do you? I researched Briarwych very carefully. It's just a nice, normal little village. The biggest danger here is boredom. And that's why I think it's best if you stay for now."

"I can't."

"Running away won't make it hurt any less."

"I'm not running away! I just don't want to be here!"

"Mr. and Mrs. Neill also want you to stay," she continues. "I know it's going to be difficult, but I really have nowhere else to place you right now, Mark. If you can just stick it out for the rest of the one month trial, and then we can reassess the situation and make a decision. Do you think you'll be able to do that for me?"

I want to tell her that I can't stay, that I *won't*, but for a moment I feel as if I'll burst into tears if I speak. I wait, and then – by the time I feel like I can say something – I've started to realize that maybe I can stick it out after all. I don't want to look like I'm scared, and she's probably right when she suggests that I'd be running away. It's just that this house feels empty without Kerry around.

"I'll stay if you can do one thing," I say finally. "Promise me that she didn't die because of what we did last night. Please, Mrs. Trevor. I'll stay, but only if you promise me that."

"I promise," she says, before placing a hand on my shoulder. "What happened to Kerry was a tragedy, that's all. It had nothing whatsoever to do with the church. I mean, come on, let's be sensible for a moment. How could the church have done anything to her?"

CHAPTER NINE
MARK

"SO YOU'RE STAYING WITH Brian and his missus, are you?"

I sort of half-smile as I set the milk and loaf on the counter. I only came out to the corner-shop to be helpful, and to get out of that pressure-cooker house for a few minutes, and I really didn't want to attract any attention. I just want people to leave me alone.

"I heard what happened," the man continues as he scans the milk and puts it into a bag. "Terrible, just terrible. How old was she?"

"Fifteen."

He winces.

"That's too young," he says, and then he scans the bread. "What was it, her heart?"

"We don't know yet."

"Must've been something like that," he mutters. "Unless... There's no chance she was on drugs, is there?"

"No," I say firmly.

"You never know these days," he adds with a sigh, before ringing up the total. "That'll be two pounds and sixty-five of your finest pence, thank you."

I start counting out the exact money from the change Mrs. Neill gave me.

"Do you mind if I give you some advice?" he asks suddenly.

I glance at him.

"Don't do anything," he adds.

"What do you mean?"

"I mean don't *do* anything while you're here. Obviously you've got to *do* things, but don't do anything big or unusual. People don't like that in Briarwych. Just get on with your day-to-day, keep your head down, and don't do anything to attract attention. Are you old enough to go for a pint in the pub?"

I shake my head.

"Pity, that'd straighten you out." He takes the coins and starts putting them into the till. "Just take my word for it, lad. Mind your own business, and others'll mind theirs." He leans toward me. "And just so you know, Gary in the Hog and Bucket won't be averse to letting you have the odd beer, so long as you behave yourself. You should pop in one evening. That way, you'll learn what it's alright to talk about round these parts, and what's best left ignored."

"Right," I reply, not really understanding what he means. It's almost like he's warning me off something. "Cheers."

Grabbing the bag, I head to the door.

"And I'm sorry about your friend," he adds.

"She wasn't my friend," I say, stopping and glancing back at him. "I didn't really know her very well at all."

***

As I make my way along the darkening street, with the bag of groceries in my arms, I can't help glancing toward the treeline and – in particular – at the spire of the church as it rises high against the late afternoon sky. The air's so cold, I can see my breath, but I keep my eyes fixed on the church as I think back to how dark and cold it was inside.

I keep hearing my words going round and round in my head.

"She wasn't my friend. I didn't really know her very well at all."

I mean, technically that's true, but for some reason I really feel like I miss her. It's stupid, of course, to miss someone you barely knew, but I just can't shake the feeling. And I can't help thinking back to that look on her face just as she was about to collapse. I could see something in her eyes, like fear maybe. I was watching her, and she furrowed her brow as if she was confused by something, and then her eyes widened in shock, and then she was gone.

She just slumped down, like somebody had flicked a switch, and that was the end of her. I know Caroline tried to revive her, and I totally get that, but now I reckon Kerry was gone before she even hit the floor. She just died right there on her feet, and there was nothing anyone could do about it.

Heading around the next corner, I suddenly hear laughing voices in the distance, and when I look ahead I see a warm, flickering light coming from one of the buildings. Even before I've taken another step, I realize that this must be the pub that the guy in the shop mentioned, and sure enough when I get to the window I look inside and see that there are loads of people inside, mostly gathered around the bar but also filling the booths and seats. A large fire is burning in the hearth, and for a moment I slow my pace so I can look inside. It's so loud in there, I reckon you wouldn't even be able to hear yourself think.

I definitely should not go in and try to order a pint.

***

"I hope you can handle this, son," the barman says as he sets a pint of beer in front of me. "And you swear you're old enough, yeah?"

"I just left my I.D. at home," I tell him. "Honest."

"Sure you did," he mutters. "In the extremely unlikely event that the old bill show up, make sure to duck down out of sight, alright? And behave yourself, or you'll never set foot in this establishment again."

"Thank you," I say, although my voice chooses that exact moment to squeak slightly, making me sound even younger than I am.

Rolling his eyes, the barman heads away to serve another customer.

I don't know why I came in here, except that the thought of going back to the cottage filled me with dread. It's like my thoughts haven't got anywhere else to go, so they're just filling my head more and more until it feels like my skull's swelling. I'm not even a drinker; I really wanted a Coke, but I thought I'd get laughed at so I ordered the weakest beer in the pub. As I lift the glass and prepare to take a sip, I can't help thinking that this was a waste of money, but at least it beats sitting alone in my room or slowly wandering the streets.

And maybe some beer will get rid of this feeling that my head's about to explode.

"Fancy seeing you here," a voice says suddenly.

Turning, I'm shocked to see Brian Neill smiling at me.

"Gotta go!" I blurt out, immediately heading toward the door, but he grabs my arm and pulls me back toward the bar.

"You're fine, lad," he says with a heavy sigh. "Just don't tell my wife, or she'll kill us both. And you're only having one, and make sure you chew a mint before we go back for dinner, okay? Otherwise she'll smell it on your breath."

"I'm sorry," I stammer.

"For what?"

"I dunno. Being here?"

"Don't make a habit of it," he continues, before taking a sip of his ale. "After everything that's happened today, I think we both deserve a little extra leeway. A house doesn't feel right just after someone's died in it." He pauses. "Have you ever seen someone die before?"

"Not really," I reply. "I mean, apparently I was with Mum when she died, but I was only six months old so I don't remember that."

"I'm sorry," he says.

I shrug. "Like I told you, I don't remember."

"But you still experienced it. That's got to

leave a mark."

"I don't believe in stuff like that," I tell him. "If I don't remember it, it doesn't affect me."

"Maybe," he mutters, before taking another sip. "I just can't believe that the pair of you arrived yesterday, and now Kerry's gone. She seemed like a nice girl. A little rough around the edges, but that's hardly a crime. Did you know her well?"

"Not really," I reply, as I glance along the bar and spot the lock-repair guy chatting to someone at the other end. "We were just in the same home for a while before we were sent here. To be honest, I always found Kerry pretty annoying. Wherever she went, there was always trouble around, you know?" I raise my glass to take my first sip, but then I pause for a moment. "I suppose I shouldn't say that, though. Not now that she's gone."

"The truth's the truth," he says. "There's no point hiding it. But people don't cause trouble for no reason. It's always good to consider why someone behaves the way they do."

"You mean like making excuses for them?"

"I mean like recognizing when someone's hurt, and lost. If you ask me, your friend Kerry had a pretty big defense mechanism going on."

"She wasn't my -"

I stop myself just in time.

"I saw a guy earlier," I continue, hoping to change the subject a little, "putting a new lock on the church door."

"That'll be Tim," he replies, looking briefly along the bar at the guy I met this morning, before turning to me again. "He does the general upkeep work, that sort of thing. He's the only one that will."

"Why?"

"Why what?"

"Why's the church shut?"

"It's a long story."

"How many people live in Briarwych?"

"Why do you want to know, Mark?"

"Two hundred? Three?"

"Somewhere in the middle there."

"And aren't some of them religious? Don't they want to go to church?"

"I'm sure they do, but -"

"Then why isn't the church open?" I continue. "It's not like religious organizations are short of money, is it? I bet there are smaller places that have a proper church."

"That church hasn't been open in a long time," he replies. "The last time it was open was back in the forties, during the war. I think it shut for good in 1942."

"And it's just stood there ever since? For more than seventy years?"

"Do you like football?" he asks, and now he's the one who seems to be trying to change the subject. "Maybe we could watch a -"

"So why not knock it down, then?"

"I beg your pardon?"

"If it's not being used, why not knock the church down?"

"You can't knock a church down," he replies. "That's just not right. They're historical buildings."

"So why is it just sitting there, then?" I ask. I know I'm nagging a little, but I really want to understand what's going on here. "Are you telling me that the people in this village don't want a church at all?"

"Why are you so obsessed with that church?"

"I'm not obsessed, I just..."

My voice trails off as I realize that maybe I *have* been getting a little agitated. There's just something about that church that keeps nagging at me. I guess I still can't quite accept that going there last night didn't somehow cause what happened to Kerry.

"I just want to know what's going on, that's all," I add finally. "I don't like not knowing why she died."

"The autopsy results should be with us in a day or two. Then we'll know."

"She was fine until we went into that church," I remind him. "I swear, there was nothing wrong with her until then."

Brian pauses, before downing the rest of his beer and then reaching over and taking mine from my hand. Without saying a word, he downs that too, before letting out a burp and wiping the foam from his mouth. He then reaches into his pocket and takes out a small white plastic box.

"Ignore the church," he says cautiously. "Do like the rest of us, and just pretend it's not there. That's the best thing." He drops some mints into his hand, and then he passes one to me. "And chew this. I mean what I said earlier. If she realizes we've been in here drinking, we'll be in so much bloody trouble."

"I didn't even have any!" I point out. "I didn't touch a drop!"

***

Dinner is a silent affair. Sitting at the table, eating sausages and mash with gravy, the three of us pretend to be really interested in our food, and the only sounds come from cutlery banging against the plates and our mouths as we chew. And every few seconds, I glance at the empty chair where Kerry should be sitting.

There are a million things I want to say, of course. Or rather, there are a million questions I want to ask. I doubt I'd get any straight answers, though, and somehow I feel as if I don't quite have the right to break the silence. I guess everyone's lost in their own thoughts. Caroline seems to be just staring at her food the whole time, while Brian keeps letting out little sighs that never quite lead to him actually saying something.

And I glance at Kerry's chair again, as I start to wonder why – when I never really liked her – I'm starting to miss her.

Finally I finish my food, although as I set my cutlery down I see that I'm way ahead of the others. I really don't like sitting here, but I know I have to be polite so I simply sit up straight and decide to wait.

"It's alright," Brian says, glancing at me, "you're excused, if you like."

"Are you sure?" I ask, but then I get to my feet before he has a chance to change his mind. As I push the chair back, the legs scrape loudly against the wooden floor. "Thank you for the food. It was really nice."

"My pleasure," Caroline says, looking at me with a painfully sad smile. "I'm glad you liked it."

I take my plate over to the sink and give it a rinse, before loading it into the dishwasher along with my cutlery. Then I head out to the hallway and make my way upstairs. As I reach the top, I realize I can hear Caroline and Brian talking now, and I stop for a moment to check whether I can hear what they're saying. I'm worried they might secretly think

I'm to blame for not stopping Kerry when she wanted to go out to the church.

"I heard he got a call today," Caroline is saying, "right after he fixed the lock."

"From who?" Brian asks.

"Who do you think?"

"How did they find out?"

"I suppose some busybody in the village took it upon themselves to let them know. I'm certain Tim didn't initiate anything. You know how he feels about the situation. There's no way he'd ever have wanted them to -"

"Hang on," Brian says, interrupting her, and a moment later I hear the kitchen door being pushed shut. I guess whatever they're talking about, they think I'm too young to know. Too much of a child.

It's like this whole village is hiding something.

CHAPTER TEN
MARK

I SCREAM AS LOUD as I can, screaming into the rushing wind as I pedal furiously along the runway with my shirt flapping all around me.

For a moment, nothing else matters. I even feel as if I'm leaving the world behind, as if I'm going so fast that all my thoughts of Kerry can't keep up. So long as I just keep pedaling, I can outrun everything that makes me feel bad and no-one can ever make me stop. I just want to be like this forever, because then I won't have to think ever again.

I pedal until I feel like my legs are about to fall off and I scream until all the air is out of my lungs and then I scream some more. And then, finally, I screech to a halt with just a few meters before the grass begins, and I put my left foot down to steady myself as I spin the bike around and look back the way I just came. I'm so out of breath, I have to lean down for a moment against the handlebars.

The runway stretches out ahead. From here, it looks as if it goes all the way to the horizon. And all around, for at least a couple of miles in every direction, the rough and featureless grassland reaches away from the concrete toward distant patches of forest. It's almost like being on a different world.

I woke up early this morning and asked Caroline if I could borrow one of the bikes. Then I came out and explored the forest, just to get away from everything for a few hours. Eventually I came across a collapsed fence, and I discovered the old, abandoned airbase that I'd already heard about. There are a few derelict old buildings nearby, but the coolest thing is this long, empty runway. I guess planes used to land and take off from this place back in the day, but now it looks like no-one has been out here for years. Which is just fine by me, because at least in a place like this no-one can hear me screaming my head off. It's my own private place, somewhere I can come to escape from everything.

Now that I've got my breath back and my heart has stopped racing, I'm ready for another go, so I set off and start pedaling as hard as I can. This time the wind is behind me, pushing me on, and I swear I'm going faster than ever as I once again start screaming.

Fuck the rest of the world.

***

"Cool," I whisper as I lean closer and take a look at another of the photos that have been left behind on the wall.

This particular picture shows a load of men standing in uniform, outside somewhere. I reckon they must be from the Second World War, and they've got that kind of pose that makes it look like they're not used to having their photo taken. Behind them there's some kind of old plane, just a small one for one or two people, and I can't help feeling total respect for the fact that they were probably preparing to hop into their planes and go off to fight in the war. Beyond the plane, there's a small, squat building, and after a moment I realize that it looks like the same building I'm standing in right now.

At the bottom of the picture, there's some scribbly writing that I find quite hard to read.

"Something Bolton," I whisper, "and the men of..."

There are some numbers, and then a load more names.

Looking over at another picture, I see that it shows one of the men from the first, standing with one hand raised in a salute. He looks really cool and confident, like he knows what he's doing and he believes with absolute conviction in the medals he's wearing on his chest. It must be nice to really believe in something like that. At the bottom, in neater writing, is that name again. Bolton.

I take a step back, and then I copy the salute that he's doing.

"Respect," I say, trying to stand like a proper soldier for a moment. I even fix my posture, straightening my back the way the soldiers are doing in all these old photos. "Duffley, Mark, reporting for -"

Suddenly I hear a rustling sound coming from somewhere nearby, and I turn to look over my shoulder.

The door is open, leading out into a corridor, and the rustling sound continues for a few more seconds before fading away. I know it's crazy, but it *sounded* like someone moving about under a bunch of bed-sheets, and sure enough a moment later I hear a faint creaking sound, as if someone's shifting their weight on a bed. I start to feel the hairs stand up on the back of my neck, because I know that there's not supposed to be anyone else out here, but then I remind myself that an abandoned place like this is probably heaving with rats and other animals.

"Hello?" I call out, just in case.

I wait, but now the place is silent again.

"Hey, yo, is anyone here?"

Silence.

"If this is just someone messing around," I continue, "then knock it off. I'm not in the mood for this kind of dumb shit."

Once I'm sure that I'm alone, I take another look around this abandoned old office. There are a few documents on one of the tables, although the words have faded away, but for the most part this place is just a massive collection of dust and grime. Someone left an old map on one of the desks, and I recognize the shape of southern England, although I don't know what all the marks and numbers mean.

There's a big window at the far end of the room, overlooking the runway, and I stand there for a moment and try to imagine what it must have been like when this place was in use. I reckon I'd have been really useful in the war. Not that I'm glorifying fighting or anything like that, but when you've got to fight for your country, that's what you do. I'd have been right here, giving orders, or I'd have been out there in one of those planes. Sometimes I think I'd be good in the army. You get told what to do in the army. You don't have to figure it out for yourself.

Smiling at my own stupid thoughts, I turn

and head out into the corridor, and then back toward the door that leads outside. I feel up for a few more bike races along that runway.

"I need a priest," a voice gasps suddenly.

I turn and look over toward an open door at the far end of the corridor.

"Please," the voice continues, sounding raspy and agonized, as if the person on the other side of the door can barely speak at all. "Fetch a priest."

Then there's that creaking sound again, like someone moving on a bed.

I hesitate for a moment, before hurrying along the corridor and stopping in the doorway. As I get there, the creaking sound stops, and I'm left looking through at an old bed that's pushed against the far wall. There's no-one on the bed, however, and when I look behind the door I realize that there's definitely no-one in the room. This is where the voice was coming from, I'm certain, and after a moment I feel a ripple of dread in my chest as I take a step back. Then, spotting an old cupboard against the far wall, I head over and pull it open, to prove to myself that no-one's hiding here.

Turning, I can't help looking at the bed. I still don't see anyone there, but somehow in my mind's eye I feel like there *should* be someone. I don't know who the person is, but he's hurt really bad, with burns all over his body, and it's like I can feel his pain. It's almost like I remember him being there, even though I've never been here before in my life.

After a moment I realize there's a weird smell in the room too, and it smells exactly like I'd imagine burned human flesh to smell. There's fear, too, lingering in the air. I can *feel* the fear, but it's not mine. It's as if someone else's fear has been left behind and now I'm breathing it in. It's getting stronger, too, and after a moment I reach my hand out and move it through the air, half-expecting to somehow feel something in the room. Finally, realizing that this room feels way too freaky, I turn to leave.

"Please," the voice gasps suddenly.

I freeze in the doorway, with my back to the bed.

"I need a priest," the voice whimpers. "Won't somebody fetch me a priest?"

I tell myself to turn and look, to prove to myself that there's nobody there, but I can't quite bring myself to move. It's as if I'm frozen here, too scared to turn around.

"I have to see a priest," the voice continues, "before..."

He lets out a low, guttural groan.

"Before..."

I try again to turn, but my body just won't obey. It's as if I'm locked in position.

"Father," the voice whispers, "I don't want to die. Please, I'm so scared. Tell me it'll be alright. Tell me it's not just emptiness and nothingness forever, tell me it's not just -"

Suddenly he screams.

Startled, I finally turn and look again at the bed. There's nobody there, but for a fraction of a second the scream still rings in my ears.

As if it was really here.

Looking around, I try to figure out what just happened. If this is someone's idea of a joke, then they sure as hell managed to play me, but somehow I don't think that voice was coming from a hidden speaker. It was right here in the room, it was a real person, but at the same time I can see for myself that there's no-one around. I swear I felt someone, though. I felt a presence, almost like a ghost. Fortunately, I'm not dumb enough to believe in that kind of shit.

I stare at the bed for a moment longer, before turning and hurrying back toward the way out. Fuck this place. I'm just getting jumpy, that's all. It's all Kerry's fault. She showed up, caused trouble and then died. I wish I'd never met her.

THE HORROR OF BRIARWYCH CHURCH

CHAPTER ELEVEN
MARK

Two weeks later

"THERE YOU ARE AGAIN," Mr. Mynot says as I stop my bike and take his paper from my bag, "right on time. I've never known a more punctual paperboy in all my life."

"It's nothing," I reply, passing the rolled-up newspaper to him. "I'm just doing my job."

"But you're doing it *well*, and that's the important thing," he says, as he unrolls the local paper and look at the front page. "That'll hold you in good stead for later life, whatever you decide to do. Unlike the idiots who run this rag. They wouldn't know what really goes on around here, not even if the truth ran up and bit them on their rumps."

Turning the paper around, he shows me a headline about a supermarket planning application that was recently turned down in one of the nearby towns. There's a photo of some people in a car park, and they look like they've chained themselves to a tree.

"I suppose nothing much happens round here," I suggest.

"And what makes you think that?"

"Well..." I pause, trying to pick my words with care so that I don't seem rude. "I just mean, Briarwych doesn't seem like the busiest place in the world. It's kinda... sleepy."

"That's what a lot of people think," he replies. "It might look quiet from the outside, but there's more going on here than you might realize. You just have to look beyond the frivolous stories that get printed on the front page of the local rag."

"What kind of things are going on?"

He pauses, before sighing. "Silly old men talking nonsense in the street, for one. Thank you for the paper, young man. I look forward to reading it from cover to cover, and learning all about local fetes and charity days."

"I should get going," I tell him with a faint smile. "See you next week."

I start cycling away. I've only got a few more deliveries to make today, and so far my second week of work has been going pretty well. I'm well ahead of schedule, which means I should be able to get home early. Sure, I wasn't too excited when Caroline told me there was a part-time delivery job going at the corner-shop, but at least it gives me something to do, and I'm managing to save all the money I make. All thirty pounds a week, but still, it's more than I had when I arrived here. And as I cycle up the hill and toward Mrs. Arnesbury's house, I can't help thinking that maybe I wouldn't mind sticking around here in Briarwych after my first month is up. If the Neills still want me here, that is. That's far from guaranteed. I need to make myself more useful around the place.

Hearing voices shouting, I glance to my left, and then I slow the bike and come to a stop as I see that two men are standing in the cemetery, arguing in front of the church's closed door.

One of the men is Tim Murphy. I didn't know his name when I first met him two weeks ago, back on the morning when he was putting a new lock on the door. Since then, I've come to learn that it's his job to deal with any matters concerning the church, although for the most part this seems to simply involve him watching to make sure that nobody goes near the place. He always seems so dour and annoyed with life, and I've actually started to feel sorry for him. One thing I've never seen him do, however, is get into an argument, and it's quite a surprise to hear that he's now really raising his voice as he talks to this other man.

The other man, meanwhile, is someone I've never seen before in my life. He's younger than Tim, maybe in his late thirties or early forties, and he's slightly taller than him too. For some reason, something about him makes me think that he's come here from somewhere far away. I can't really hear his voice too well, and overall he looks to be much calmer than Tim. As I ease my bike over toward the wall so I can try to listen to the argument, I can't help noticing that Tim is gesticulating wildly with his hands while the new man is simply shaking his head and gesturing repeatedly toward the door.

"I won't have someone coming and telling me how to handle this!" Tim is shouting angrily. "Nobody asked you to come here and interfere!"

The other man says something, but he speaks softly and I can't make out any of the words.

"Over my dead body!" Tim snaps. "I don't care who turns up, I'm not allowing it. Everything's been fine here for seventy-odd years. We know how to handle the situation and you don't have the authority to come here and start giving orders. Now get the hell out of this cemetery, and get the hell out of this village!"

There's a pause, and then the man says something in response before turning and walking toward the gate. As he goes, he glances this way and we briefly make eye contact. Turning, I set off again on my bike, but I stop at the next corner and look back once more. The man is now out of view, and I watch as Tim checks the lock on the church's door. Even from here, I can tell that he's angry about something. He's scowling, and I think he's even talking to himself, and then finally he turns and starts stomping over to the gate.

I don't know who that man was, but it's clear that he managed to make Tim Murphy absolutely furious.

***

As I open the front door, I hear voices coming from the kitchen. It's not until I've shut the door and started taking off my coat, however, that I realize I only recognize one of the voices. Caroline's in there, but she sounds stressed and a moment later I hear an unfamiliar male voice speaking to her very softly and calmly. Whoever she's talking to, it's certainly not Brian.

I hesitate for a moment, before heading to the doorway and looking through, and to my surprise I see that Caroline is talking to the same man I saw earlier in the cemetery. He was arguing with Tim Murphy back then, and now he seems to be upsetting Caroline. She's just about to say something to him, but then she freezes as soon as she spots me, and she looks horrified that I'm home early.

"Mark, can you go to your room, please?" she snaps. "Now."

"What's wrong?" I ask.

"Nothing, just go to your room. I'll let you know when you can come down."

"You must be Mark Duffley," the man says, stepping toward me with an outstretched hand. "I'm -"

"Don't shake his hand, Mark," Caroline says sternly.

I open my mouth to ask again what's wrong, but now I'm starting to feel really creeped out. Caroline looks like she's close to tears, while the strange man is staring at me.

"Go to your room," Caroline says again. "That's an order, Mark."

"I think the boy's old enough to make his own decisions," the man says. "Mark, I'd like to talk to you about -"

"Enough!" Caroline shouts, before rushing over and pushing me back out into the hallway. "Go to your room!" she says firmly, as if she's on the verge of some kind of meltdown. I think there are even tears in her eyes. "Now! No arguments, just go!"

Shocked by her demeanor, I pause for a moment and then I do as I'm told. Turning, I head to the stairs and then up to the landing, and as I reach the halfway point I hear the kitchen door being slammed shut. By the time I get to the top of the stairs I can hear Caroline raising her voice in the kitchen, and it sounds as if she's really giving this man a piece of her mind. Honestly, she's usually so quiet and polite, so it's a real surprise to hear her getting so angry and animated down there. I can't imagine what could do this to her.

I make my way over to my bedroom, but then I stop as I hear the kitchen door opening again. Footsteps move toward the front door, and then I hear that open as well.

"If you change your mind," the man says calmly, "I'll be at the Hog and Bucket for at least the rest of the week. I'm not trying to cause trouble here, Mrs. Neill. Quite the opposite. Containment isn't working, and sooner or later the people of this village need to accept that there's a -"

"Leave my house now, please," she says firmly.

"It's only -"

"Get out of my house. Now. Before I call the authorities and have you removed."

There's a pause, and then I hear the front door swinging shut, leaving the house in silence. And then, a few seconds later, I hear Caroline starting to sob.

My first instinct is to go down and ask if

she's okay, but somehow I feel as if she probably wants to be left alone. Besides, it's not as if she'd actually tell me what's wrong. Over the past couple of weeks, I've noticed her having several hushed, secretive conversations with her husband, and the conversations always stop as soon as they realize that I'm around. I've never managed to overhear what they're talking about, and when I ask they just say that there's nothing for me to worry about. They treat me like a child who has no right to know the truth.

Heading into my room, I go over to the window and look out. At first I look at the spire of the church, but then I look down and spot movement in the street. The man is walking away from the cottage, heading back toward town. He's already upset two people here in Briarwych this morning, which makes me really wonder who he is and why he's here. Whatever it is, I reckon it must be linked to the way everyone whispers around here and acts like they're keeping some big secret.

I guess there's only one way I'm ever going to find out what's really going on here in Briarwych.

CHAPTER TWELVE
MARK

MY FIRST STROKE OF luck is that when I arrive at the Hog and Bucket, there's no sign of Brian. Based on Caroline's reaction to the strange visitor earlier, I'm pretty sure that Brian would haul me out of here as soon as he spotted me. And my seconds stroke of luck is that, as I slip through the crowd and make my way to the bar, I spot the strange man eating at a corner table.

I don't go straight over. Instead, I go to the bar and order a Coke, and then I watch as the man continues to eat. He's wearing all black, which is something I hadn't noticed before, and there's something very calm about him. I can just about see his plate, and he seems to be eating from left to right. There's something strangely fascinating about this guy, and I can't help staring at him for a few minutes until, finally, he wipes his mouth on a napkin and then gets to his feet.

I immediately look down at my drink, in case I'm spotted, but out of the corner of my eye I can see the man heading through to the corridor that leads to the beer garden. I glance around, to make doubly certain that Brian's not here, and then I slip through the crowd of drinkers and head along the corridor myself. I don't even know what I want to say to this guy, but I guess I just want to hear why he's here.

Reaching the back door, I pull it open and step out into the beer garden, but to my surprise there's no-one out there. I glance around for a moment, trying to figure out where the man might have gone, and then I shut the door before turning to go back to the bar.

"Hello, Mr. Duffley," the man says as I almost slam straight into him. "Shall we talk in my room?"

***

"And what exactly did your friend say while she was sitting on the altar?" Liam asks, as he makes some more notes in his journal. "Do you remember the exact words she used?"

"Not the exact words," I reply, "just... She

kept asking me why I was in the church, which is stupid 'cause she knew why. And she said it was *her* church, which didn't make sense either."

He makes some more notes.

"But I still don't get why you're asking me about all this," I continue. "Kerry was sick, but it wasn't to do with anything in that church. It was just a coincidence that we were in there the night before." I wait for him to agree with me, but he's simply writing more and more notes. "Are you a priest?" I add finally.

"Hmm?"

He glances at me, and for a moment he looks a little puzzled by the question.

"Oh," he continues, "yes, I am. I mean, among other things. I have been a priest, but now my day-to-day activities are a little different."

"Are you from, like, the Pope or someone?" I ask.

He furrows his brow. "The Pope?"

"Yeah. Did the Pope send you? 'Cause it's a church, and I guess we broke in, so maybe the Pope heard and he's sent you to sort it out."

"Briarwych Church comes under the authority of the Anglican community in this country," he replies. "It's not a Catholic institution."

"Oh." I pause, trying to work out what he means. "So are you and the Pope not in the same group?"

"I work for an organization that has links to a great many institutions and faiths," he explains calmly. "Irrespective of my personal background, I'm mindful of the needs of all Christians, regardless of their denominations. I'm also in regular touch with leading figures from other religious groups, such as Judaism and Islam and Hinduism. We all have certain things in common."

"Right," I reply, even though I still don't quite understand. "So who actually owns the church in Briarwych?"

"The people who have asked me to come here."

"Right." I pause. "So they sent you because we broke in? You're not going to call the police, are you? I'll pay for the lock, I swear, and we didn't take anything. Well, Kerry took a bag, but you can have that back."

"Nobody's going to contact the police," he replies. "If somebody did, they'd immediately get in touch with yours truly."

"Who's mine truly?"

"Me, Mark," he explains. "I meant that they'd refer the situation directly to me. Or at least to one of my superiors, who in turn would send me to investigate. And I can assure you that the loss of a lock on an old wooden door is of no real interest to me whatsoever." He pauses again, watching me with that same calm demeanor that I first noticed back at the cottage. "What do you know about the church at Briarwych?"

"I looked it up on Google," I tell him.

"What did you find?"

"Nothing much."

"Good. We've worked very hard to keep it that way."

"What's going on with that church?" I ask, unable to hold back my exasperation any longer. "Why do people talk about it like that?"

"Like what?"

"The way *you* just did. Like everyone's hiding something!"

"You're a very perceptive young man."

"Don't patronize me!"

He takes a deep breath.

"The church here in Briarwych has been closed since 1942," he explains finally. "Not a single living soul set foot inside the place for more than three quarters of a century, until the night you and your friend entered the building."

"Why?" I ask.

"The church was sealed."

"Why? Why have you all been trying to stop people getting in?"

I wait, but he looks concerned.

"Or are you..."

My voice trails off for a moment.

"Are you trying to stop something getting

out?" I ask, before realizing how ridiculous that idea is. It's so ridiculous, in fact, that I immediately get to my feet. "I think I'm gonna go now," I tell him. "Sorry, but I'm not into all this weird shit."

Turning, I head toward the door.

"She killed your friend," Liam says suddenly. "She killed Kerry."

I stop and look back over at him.

"I'm sorry," he continues, "but there's no doubt about that whatsoever."

"What are you talking about?" I ask.

"You said it yourself, Mark. While you were in the church, Kerry started acting strangely. She referred to a woman she'd seen and heard. She herself said strange things. She suffered a brief, temporary possession while she was sitting on that altar."

"Possession?" I reply, barely able to believe that he's coming out with this stuff. "Are you for real?"

"The autopsy stated that she died due to an aneurysm," he continues. "While that isn't strictly a contradiction of the truth, the aneurysm itself was caused by mounting pressure in Kerry's cranium. Your friend was murdered as an act of revenge. She was killed by a cruel, vengeful entity that has been allowed to fester inside that church for far too long."

"That church was empty," I point out.

He shakes his head.

"There was no-one there!" I continue, raising my voice even though I didn't mean to. "Kerry was rambling on about someone, but that's just because she was crazy! And if you think there was someone in there with us, then maybe you're crazy too!"

Sighing, he gets to his feet. He steps past me, and then he takes his jacket from a hook on the wall. As he begins to put the jacket on, he also reaches into one of the pockets and removes something small.

"Where are you going?" I ask.

"Where do you think?" He shows me a small metal key with a strange design. "I'm going to the church."

"But you're not -"

"The act of authorization, enacted by the late Bishop Alfred Carmichael in 1942, permits any representative of the Council to enter the church at Briarwych," he replies calmly, almost as if he'd anticipated what I was about to say. "Locks be damned, Mark. I need to see the interior of that place for myself, before I decide how to proceed. And to be perfectly frank with you, I've lost patience with the petty superstition of people here in the village. Nobody has the legal or moral right to keep me out of the church, and I'm done with the niceties."

With that, he opens the door and steps out into the corridor, before glancing back at me.

"So," he adds finally, "are you coming with me?"

CHAPTER THIRTEEN
MARK

"YOU WON'T EVEN GET the door open," I tell Liam as I follow him through the undergrowth that fills the cemetery. "Mate, I've seen the lock on that door. It's ten times stronger than the one Kerry managed to break."

"I very much doubt that your friend broke anything," he says, reaching the door and sliding his own key into Tim's lock. He struggles for a moment, before managing to click the key into place. "That lock was opened from the inside."

"No, she -"

Before I can finish, there's another loud clicking sound and part of Tim's lock falls away. Liam quickly pulls the metal plate aside, before turning the ring-pull thing on the front of the door.

Then, stepping back, he pulls the door open to reveal the gloomy interior.

Feeling an instant chill, I take a step back as I see the gray stone walls of the church's main corridor. Last time I was here, it was too dark to see anything at all.

I open my mouth to tell this Liam guy that he's tripping balls, but then something stops me. I can't help staring into the church, and once again I get this really strong feeling that somehow something's staring back at me. I can see the corridor, I can even see the wall at the far end, and there's blatantly no-one there. At the same time, I swear I can feel a pair of eyes watching me, and the sensation builds and builds until finally I feel like I just want to run and not look back.

"Tell me what you're thinking right now," Liam says.

I turn to him.

"Are you feeling something?" he continues. "Maybe something you can't quite explain?"

"I'm feeling embarrassed, mate," I reply, unable to drop the defensiveness. "For you. You're nuts."

"Am I?" He pauses, before pushing the door all the way open and then taking a step into the church. "Well, I suppose there's only one way to -"

"Stop!" I blurt out.

He turns to me.

"I didn't mean that," I add, even though I'm shocked by my own reaction. Seeing Liam entering the church reminded me of when Kerry went inside, and the thought of that moment has sent me into a kind of panic. "I don't think you should go in there, that's all."

"I was under the impression that you don't believe what I told you back in my room."

"I don't, but -"

"So go home," he continues, cutting me off. "It's been very interesting to talk to you, Mark, but I'm not going to force you to come into the church with me. Go home. Be like all the others in Briarwych. Pretend nothing's happening here, pretend the evil in this church can be contained forever by a wooden door and a fancy lock. Pretend your friend Kerry died of a random aneurysm. Lie to yourself. It's easier."

Turning, he starts walking along the corridor. His steps ring out as he advances into the gloom, and as I watch him I have to really fight the urge to yell at him and to tell him he's making a mistake.

"Not again," I whisper under my breath, still thinking back to the night here with Kerry. "Come on, this is too much."

I should leave, like he said, but somehow I stay right here for a moment. I can still see Mark, even though the church's interior is pretty shadowy, and he's getting closer and closer to the far end of the corridor. That's where the feeling of being watched is coming from, and I can't shake the fear that he's walking straight toward something that shouldn't be there. And even though I want to get out of here, I finally take a step forward into the doorway, and then I make my way into the church. People have called me a lot of things over the years, but the only thing I really hate is being called a coward.

I'm shaking, though, and I don't know whether that's because of how cold it is in here, or because of the way some invisible gaze seems to be burning into me.

"Can we just go?" I ask, unable to keep the fear from my voice. "I can't just leave you here, but can we go?"

He doesn't reply. Instead, as he reaches the end of the corridor he turns and starts carefully taking something from one of the other pockets of his jacket.

"This place is creepy as shit," I continue, stepping along the corridor, forcing myself to keep going. The last thing I want is to be here, but at the same time I'm not going to let this Liam guy think that he's managed to scare me. I'm going to prove to him, and to myself, that there's nothing bad here. "You're wasting your time."

Stopping halfway along the corridor, I see

that he's holding a small glass vial of liquid.

"What's that?" I ask cautiously.

"Do you sense her, Mark?" he replies.

"Sense who?"

"The woman your friend Kerry encountered that night while she was sitting on the altar." He slowly swings the vial from the end of a short silver chain. "Her name is, or was, Judith Prendergast."

"There's no-one here," I point out, although at that moment I can't help looking past Liam and watching the space behind him. I tell myself I'm imagining things, but at the same time I feel like there's something invisible in the air, something that's just past his left shoulder.

"Don't worry," Liam continues, watching the vial as he turns, as if he expects it to suddenly start swinging differently, "she won't appear right now. She's cautious by nature. Not as cautious as she was seventy years ago, but still cautious, especially when she knows that there's a man of the cloth here."

He turns again, as the vial continues to swing.

"I'm certain that she's close, though," he adds, turning again. "She'll be drawn to us, to see who we are and why we -"

"Stop!" I yell, as he turns to face the space right behind him. At that moment, the vial suddenly starts swinging wildly in the other direction.

Liam takes a step back and looks at the far end of the corridor.

"She's definitely here," he continues, before glancing at me. "You sense her, Mark, don't you?"

"I don't know what you're talking about!" I snap, watching as the vial continues to swing far more wildly than before. "You're doing that with your fingers."

"She must be right here," he says, watching the far wall. "She's close, as close as she dares to come." He starts backing away, coming closer to me as the vial begins to swing more normally again. "After seventy years alone, she must be pretty surprised to have visitors. Then again, she's been waiting for that door to be breached, maybe even learning how to open it herself from the inside." He stops next to me, and now the vial is simply hanging from the chain. "She wants to know what we want here."

Stopping, he crouches down and look at a spot at the bottom of the archway. There looks to be some kind of mark carved into stonework, and he runs a fingertip against the surface for a moment before getting back to his feet.

"What is that thing?" I ask, looking at the vial and seeing that it contains a small amount of what seems to be water.

"Just a few drops of holy water," he replies. "I'm confident that we're safe for the moment, but it's always good to have some insurance."

"Holy water?" I ask. "For real? Isn't that just... normal water?"

"You saw how it reacted in her presence."

"Yeah, but that was you playing with it."

"I assure you, I did nothing," he replies, still watching the wall at the corridor's far end for a moment, before turning to me. "She's here with us, Mark. The ghost of Judith Prendergast is right here in this space, and she's watching us."

***

"What happened here, anyway?" I ask a few minutes later, as Liam begins to make his way along the aisle. "Did someone trash this place?"

Stopping in the archway, I look at the ruined pews, which looks like they were set on fire a long time ago. A moment later I glance over my shoulder, looking back along the corridor. I still feel like I'm being watched, like something's at the corridor's far end, but I keep telling myself to stop being such a wimp. Looking back over at Mark, I see that he's reached the altar, and I feel a flicker of fear as I remember the way Kerry sat up there on that thing.

"Hey!" I call out, making my way along the aisle and then stopping as I get halfway. "Why are all these chairs so trashed?"

He turns to me. He's still holding the vial, which is hanging still.

"There was a fire," he explains. "It wasn't exactly an accident. According to Father Loveford's testimony, the fire was started deliberately but then extinguished a short while later, before any real structural damage could be done. Of course, by the time of that testimony the church had already been re-sealed, and nobody was very keen to come in and remove the debris." He looks around at the ruined pews. "They've stood like this for more than seventy years. They're another form of testimony, I suppose. They're a reminder of what happened the last time people came into this church."

"Who set it on fire?" I ask cautiously.

"A very troubled young woman."

"But why?"

"Because she was misguided," he continues. "The ghost of Judith Prendergast was directing her. Encouraging her. The ghost wasn't as strong then as it is now, but it still almost managed to trap an entire congregation and have them burn to death. I suppose the ghost has had plenty of time to reflect upon her failure to -"

Suddenly there's a scraping sound in the distance. Turning, I look back toward the archway, but I don't see anything. Somehow I know, however, that I'll feel like I'm begin watched again if I go and look back along the corridor.

"Maybe she doesn't like being reminded of those times," Liam continues as I turn to him again. "Maybe she's a little sensitive about it all."

"You're talking about her like she's..."

My voice trails off for a moment.

"Like she's real," I add finally. "Like she's really here, like ghosts are real."

"You don't have to believe me," he replies. "I can't force you. But I think deep down you know I'm right, otherwise you wouldn't have followed me back in here today. And you can feel things, Mark, can't you? Tell me, on the night you first came here, did your friend Kerry show any sign of fear before she started acting strangely?"

I pause, before shaking my head.

"I'm sure she felt something," he adds, "but it would have been weak enough for her to dismiss it. That's how most people are in this kind of location. But you picked up on something, didn't you?"

"I thought it was stupid to be here," I tell him. "I still do."

"Are you sure that's why you were being so cautious?"

"It was cold and I was tired!"

"But there was something else, wasn't there?"

"You know what?" I add, feeling beyond frustrated. "Screw this pile of -"

Suddenly I feel something brushing against the back of my neck. Turning, I instinctively take a step back, and for a moment I feel filled with a burst of fear. It's not like I feel that I'm being watched right now; instead, it's like I can feel something moving past me, making its way along the aisle. For a fraction of a second that sensation is palpable, it's so strong I think I might faint, but then it begins to subside and I'm left looking toward Liam as he remains on the altar with the vial hanging from his fingers.

"What was that?" he asks. "What did you feel?"

"Nothing," I stammer.

"It didn't look like nothing."

"It was just..." I take a deep breath and try to sort myself out. "You can't blame me for being freaked out!" I point out finally. "Kerry died after being here, and now you're telling a load of bullshit ghost stories! Anyone'd be bothered by stuff like that!"

I wait, but now he's simply watching the vial.

"It's so easy to get scared even though there's nothing to be scared of!" I continue. "I get that, it's human nature. You spout a load of bollocks about a ghost, and of course people are gonna get their panties in a twist, but that doesn't mean any of it's real! It just means that -"

Before I can finish, I see that the vial is starting to swing again. Only gently, but enough for me to notice from over here.

"It just means that you're good at fucking with people," I stammer, "and with their minds, and -"

I stop as the vial's swing becomes stronger. Maybe even stronger than before. Still, it's blatantly obvious that Liam's controlling it with his fingers. He's probably as much a magician as he is a priest.

"You're clever," I add, "I'll give you that, but..."

My voice trails off as the vial suddenly swings to the right and then hovers there, as if it's being repulsed by something on the other side of Liam's hand. I want to tell him that I don't believe in any of this, but when I look at his face I see that he's staring down at the vial with a hint of fear in his eyes, and I realize he's whispering something very quietly. Instinctively, I take a step forward, and as I do so I swear I feel the air getting colder against my face.

I can hear Liam's voice a little better now. I can make out the words he's saying, but I don't know what any of them mean. He's speaking in some kind of foreign language, and slowly his voice is filling with more and more tension. The vial, meanwhile, is trembling harder than ever, and it's still hanging way to one side.

"What are you doing?" I ask finally, taking another step forward.

I wait, but he doesn't say anything. At the same time, I can feel my chest tightening with fear, as if somebody's grabbed my heart and has started twisting it around and around.

"Hey, come on," I continue, unable to hide my frustration for a moment longer. "You're just messing around!"

Still he says nothing. I take another step forward, even though I want to turn and run, and now the tightening sensation in my chest is so strong that I'm actually starting to feel a little breathless.

Liam is still speaking in that nonsense language.

"Hey!" I yell. "You're taking this too far!"

His hand is shaking now as he continues to hold the vial.

"Stop!" I shout.

"Amen Christus," he says through gritted teeth, almost as if he's in pain, and then he starts saying the same thing over and over again. "Amen Christus, Amen Christus, Amen -"

"Stop!" I yell.

Suddenly Liam gasps and steps back. He drops the vial in the process, letting it fall to the floor and shatter. In that same instant, the tightening knot vanishes from my chest and I feel as if the air is no longer quite so bitingly cold. I wait for Liam to say something, however, and he simply looks down at the floor and watches as some of the vial's liquid dribbles down from one step to the next.

"Well," he says finally, sounding a little shaken as he adjusts the cuffs of his jacket, "that was rather educational, wasn't it?"

Hurrying down from the space around the altar, he comes over to me and grabs my arm, and then he leads me pretty fast toward the archway that leads back into the corridor.

"I was going to explore the whole church," he explains, "but there's really no point. I think I've learned enough to be getting on with."

Stopping at the archway, he takes a small, square white patch from his pocket and peels a layer of plastic from the rear, and then he sticks the patch onto a section of the archway.

"What's that?" I ask.

"She's nervous," he explains, as he presses the patch more firmly against the stonework. "I'd like to keep her that way for as long as possible. I want to give her something to think about."

He pats the patch one more time, as if to make sure that it's properly in place, and then he grabs my arm and leads me toward the open main door.

"Let's get out of here," he continues, sounding a little flustered. "I thin I've seen just about enough for one day."

CHAPTER FOURTEEN
MARK

"WHAT EXACTLY HAPPENED BACK there?" I ask as I sit at a corner table in the busy pub, watching Liam tapping at something on his laptop. "Don't lie to me. You got pretty freaked out for a moment."

"One should never become too confident," he replies as he continues to type. "One's expectations will always be shattered eventually."

"Yeah, but -"

Before I can finish that sentence, I notice that there's some kind of red mark on Liam's right wrist. At first I assume it's a scar, but then I realize that it looks much fresher and more recent, almost as if he burned himself.

I'm about to ask him about the mark, but

then he glances at me and sees that I'm watching him. He quickly reaches down and pulls his jacket's cuff over the wound, and then he gets back to typing.

"This is almost ready," he explains. "I've got a decent signal, all thing considered. I was worried those stones would block most of it, but I'm getting it loud and clear." He grabs a set of headphones and plugs them into the side of the laptop, and then he listens for a moment before passing on of the buds to me. "Go on," he says, "don't be afraid. It won't bite."

"What am I listening to?" I ask as I put the bug in one ear and stick a finger in the other to drown out the sound of the pub.

I listen, but all I hear is a faint hissing sound.

"What is this?" I ask.

"I left a small, discreet microphone in the church," Liam explains. "Just a little device I picked up from some friends who work in the military." He clicks something on his mouse, and the hissing sound flares for a moment. "I'm not really very good at modern technology, though," he continues, "so you'll have to bear with me. I think I've more or less got it set up, though. It's just a matter of tweaking things."

"Why are you doing this?"

"Why do you think?"

Before I can reply, I hear the hissing sound start to subside.

"There," he says, "that's the feed from inside the church right now. You saw me lock the door again after we left, Mark. That place is as sealed now as it has been for the past seventy years. There's nothing and nobody in there. Well, apart from the obvious."

"So what are you, exactly?" I ask. "Some kind of ghost-busting priest?"

"No, I -"

Suddenly he pauses for a moment.

"Did you hear that?" he asks.

I listen to the earbud, but all I hear is that consistent, faint hiss.

"So that was all an act back in the church, wasn't it?" I continue. "With the vial, I mean. I get it, you have to dress this stuff up and make it more theatrical." I wait for him to admit that I'm right, but he seems far more focused on listening to the stupid hissing sound. "It was kind of impressive," I add finally. "I mean, you're pretty good at this stuff. You should be on the telly. Have you ever thought about going on *Britain's Got Talent*?"

"I can hear her," he replies.

"Exactly," I continue, "you're really -"

Before I can finish, I realize I heard something as well. The hissing sound is still there, but I heard a faint shuffling noise coming over the signal, as if something or somebody brushed against one of the stone walls. I immediately tell myself that I imagined the whole thing, but then I hear it again and this time it sounds a little closer.

"Imagine spending seventy-plus years all alone in that place," Liam says after a few seconds. "You'd know every inch of it by heart. Every crack and crevice. And then if somebody came and changed something, or added something, it'd seem like the most exciting thing ever. Plus, I doubt a woman who died in the 1940's would have any clue about what I stuck on that wall. To her, a microphone would be a big, bulky item."

"So you're trying to attract her attention?" I ask. "Is that really a good idea?"

"I need to keep her guessing," he explains. "If she gets too confident, that's when she starts hurting people." He glances at me. "That's when people like your friend get killed."

"You make it sound like she's -"

Suddenly I hear a scratching sound coming over the earbud. I listen, trying to remind myself that this is all just bullshit anyway, but it really sounds like someone's scratching the church's stone walls.

"Okay, so there are mice in there," I say, although I can hear the fear in my own voice. "That's all this is."

"And these mice are six feet up on the side

of a stone wall, are they?" he asks. "You're going to have to do better than that."

I listen as the scratching sound continues. I keep expecting it to end. If anything, however, it seems to be getting a little louder. Or maybe just closer to the little microphone that Liam attached to the wall. And no matter how hard I try to tell myself that this whole thing is a load of rubbish, I can't help but imagine the stillness and the silence of that church, and I can't help but wonder what could be making the noise I'm hearing.

"It's a trick," I say finally, as much to convince myself as to let Liam know that I'm onto him. "It's just a -"

Suddenly a shrill voice screams over the earbud. Before I can pull away, there's a loud thudding sound and the hissing ends, and I finally manage to take the earbud out and drop it onto the table.

Turning to Liam, I see that he's already tapping at his laptop.

"What the fuck was that?" I stammer.

"I definitely got her attention," he replies, furrowing his brow as he continues to work for a moment. Finally, he stops and turns to me. "She destroyed the microphone."

"What are you talking about?"

"She destroyed it," he continues. "It's not complicated. It *is* surprising, however. I didn't think she'd be so quickly angered, or that she'd understand to destroy the thing." He pauses, and I can tell that he's shocked. "When I came here, I was worried that over the years she'd grown more dangerous that other people thought. Now I think she's grown more dangerous than even *I* thought. None of my conjectures included the possibility that she could destroy the equipment."

I open my mouth to tell him that I'm not buying it, that he can't pull the wool over my eyes quite so easily. Before I can say any of that, however, I feel a sudden flicker of fear in my chest. Something about the look of fear in Liam's eyes seems to be countering all the logic I can summon.

"Who is she?" I ask finally, even though I think I'm scared of the answer. "*What* is she?"

***

"Her name was, I mean is, I mean... Whatever. She's Judith Prendergast. She's a woman who died in that church in 1940. Her body was discovered two years later, in 1942, when Father Lionel Loveford arrived to open the place and get it up and running again."

We're back up in his room now, and he's taking some documents from a bag. There are photos and scans, although I can't really make much out, even when I crane my neck to get a better look.

"How did she die?" I ask.

"It seems that she had a run-in with Father Loveford's predecessor, a man by the name of David Perkins. For reasons that are rather unclear, Father Perkins locked Judith Prendergast in the church when he left to fight in the war. I'm sure he expected her to find her way out soon enough, but it would appear that she instead went up into the church's bell-tower. Then, somehow, she fell at the top of the stairs and hit her head, and she was subsequently found by her daughter Elizabeth once the church had reopened. Although, again, there is some question as to *when* the body was found, and whether Elizabeth had previously broken into the church and found her mother before Father Loveford's arrival."

He pauses, before sliding a copy of an old, black-and-white photo over to me.

"Back row, on the left," he says as I pick the photo up. "We're not certain, but we think that's Judith Prendergast in 1939, about a year before her death."

As soon as I see the woman's face, I flinch. She's staring intently at the camera. I know it's crazy, but I swear I feel the same way I felt back in the church when I thought I was being watched.

"By all accounts, she was an unpopular lady around these parts," he continues. "We're not certain about some aspects of her story. What happened to her husband, for example, is unclear, or even whether she had one. She had a daughter, so we assume there was a husband, but records for that period are incomplete when it comes to this area. What we *do* know is that the locals weren't particularly keen to retrieve her from the church. So much so, in fact, that nobody went to check on her."

"For how long?"

When he doesn't immediately reply, I turn to him.

"How long did they leave her in there?" I ask.

"Until Father Loveford arrived," he explains. "They collectively assumed that she'd found her way out and that, for whatever reason, she'd decided to leave Briarwych overnight. A somewhat odd assumption, I'm sure you'll agree, but you have to understand that she was really, truly reviled. Many years ago I spoke to a few people who were around at the time, and they treated her as almost a pantomime villain. By all accounts she was cruel, vindictive, hypocritical and merciless. She was so bad, indeed, that I can't help but feel there must be more to the story."

"Why?" I ask.

"Because nobody is as bad as Judith Prendergast was made out to be. At least, not in my experience. There has to have been more to her, as if..." He pauses. "Well, I'll get to that shortly. Let's just say that I have a few theories of my own."

He takes another photo from his bag and looks at it for a moment, before passing it over to me. The photo shows an elderly, white-haired man smiling cautiously at the camera while standing in a garden somewhere.

"I took that photo in 1999," he continues, "when I went to visit Father Loveford at Meadow's Downe Asylum."

"He was in an asylum?"

"Not quite. He was merely visiting. But Elizabeth Prendergast was there, and Father Loveford had become rather attached to her. So he spent almost every day sitting by her bed, waiting for her to wake up. Apart from a few necessary journeys to London, he'd arrive every morning at 8am and he'd sit there, talking to her, until he had to leave at 5pm to cycle home. Even though Elizabeth – or Lizzy, as he called her – never woke from her coma, he spent more than fifty years by her side."

"That's mental," I reply, staring at the photo of the old man. "Didn't he realize there was no point?"

"He always hoped that she'd wake up. And he said he sensed her sometimes. He was rather loathe to discuss the matter, but when I met him he told me that he thought he sometimes felt her presence in the room."

"Like a ghost?"

"Well, she wasn't dead," he points out. "She never really woke up after she arrived at the asylum."

He passes me another photo, which shows the same old man sitting in a chair, next to a woman who looks like she's asleep on a bed.

"Is that her?" I ask.

"It is."

"She seriously spent decades and decades just asleep like that?"

"Not asleep. Comatose. Damaged."

"That's crazy. And he didn't get bored sitting there with her?"

"Father Lionel Loveford died on December the first, 1999," he continues, "just a few weeks after I visited him, and after these pictures were taken."

"That's sad," I admit. "What about the woman? When did she die?"

"Elizabeth Prendergast died on the exact same day. In fact, she seems to have died at the exact same moment as Father Loveford. A nurse was in the room, talking to Lionel, and then she left to fetch some things. She returned ninety seconds later and found them both dead. They were holding hands, and it was as if they'd both just slipped away." He pauses. "If you were of a romantic disposition, Mark," he adds finally, "you might speculate that she was clinging to life, waiting for him, and that once he was gone..."

His voice trails off.

"Well," he says with a smile, as I turn to him, "I often include them in my prayers. I have hope that after everything they endured in their lives, they might have found happiness together. Wherever they are now."

"That's kinda cute," I admit, sliding the photo back to him. "A bit weird, but cute."

"Meanwhile, Judith Prendergast's ghost remained locked in the church here in Briarwych," he explains. "After the events of 1940 and 1942, the locals in the village wanted the church sealed. They hoped that this would deal with the problem once and for all. Bishop Carmichael, who was in charge at the time, agreed to their wishes, but on one proviso. He insisted that if the ghost of Judith Prendergast ever showed signs of stirring, of trying to reach beyond the church, then something would have to be done."

He passes me another photo. It's black-and-white again, and I immediately recognize the exterior of the church. Several stern-looking men are standing in the cemetery, and some of them are wearing robes that make them look like priests.

"After the events of 1942," Liam continues, "Bishop Carmichael was never happy with how Briarwych Church had been handled. I never met the man myself, but I've read his diaries from the period. He wasn't happy with the arrangement and he felt it wouldn't last forever, but he agreed to give it a try. But I believe he foresaw a day when containment would no longer work. I also believe that day has finally arrived."

"You make it sound like she's evil," I point out.

"I fear that her power is growing," he replies, "and that perhaps there's more to this situation than meets the eye. After all, the exact circumstances surrounding Judith's death have never been clear, and I'm not satisfied with the idea that this is merely an ordinary haunting. I need to be certain, though. That's why I've got a plan to determine exactly what we're dealing with."

Reaching into one of his bags, he fumbles for a moment before pulling out a large truck that's fitted with go-faster stripes. After setting the truck on the table, he reaches into the bag and this time he pulls out a remote control system.

"I can only hope that I'm wrong," he continues, "about the precise nature of the *thing* that's haunting Briarwych Church."

CHAPTER FIFTEEN
MARK

"HANG ON," LIAM SAYS as he sits cross-legged on the floor in front of the open church door, "I think I -"

Before he can finish, the remote-controlled truck races forward and slams into the side of the door.

"Why are these things so tricky to operate?" he mutters, fiddling with the controls and finally managing to make the truck reverse slightly.

"You're not doing it right," I tell him. "Why don't you let me try to -"

"There!"

He turns one of the dials, but this only causes the truck to start driving around in circles.

"What's it doing?" Liam says with a sigh.

"That's supposed to make it go forward, not round and round."

"Can you get on with it?" I ask, glancing through the open doorway and once again seeing the gloomy corridor that runs along the interior of the church. I still feel that same sense of being watched, as if someone or something is at the corridor's far end. "Drive the bloody thing inside so we can shut the door!"

"That's what I'm trying to do," he replies, "but I think these controls are broken."

"They're not broken, you're just not -"

"Okay, I think I've got it."

He adjusts another of the dials, and then he pushes a small joystick. The truck revs for a moment, before driving head-first into the wall.

"Give that to me!" I sigh, grabbing the controls from his hands. I take a look for a moment at the various buttons, and then I realize how they work. Almost immediately, I manage to reverse the truck away from the wall, and then I drive it smoothly through the open doorway and into the corridor. "Now can you please shut the door?" I ask. "It's giving me the chills."

"Fine," he mutters, before swinging the door shut and securing the lock.

Looking down at his laptop, I see that the camera feed from the truck is working perfectly, showing a view of the corridor from low down on the ground. I drive the truck forward a few meters, and then I stop it again.

"Is there really any point to this?" I ask. "Won't she just smash it, like she smashed the microphone?"

"She might," he replies, watching the video feed intently, "or she might not. Whatever she does, her reaction will be instructional." He makes a few adjustments on the laptop. "I need to know for certain what she is."

"I thought you said that already," I point out. "She's a ghost. Not that I necessarily believe you, but I thought that's what *you* believed."

"She's not acting like a ghost," he replies. "Not entirely. I'm worried that there's something we're missing."

"Like -"

"Take it forward a little way," he continues. "Not too far."

"How's a ghost supposed to act?" I ask, as I drive the truck very carefully along the corridor and then stop it again. "Is that okay?"

"That's perfect." He peers at the laptop. "Where did you sense her presence the most, Mark?"

"Me?"

"Yes. Don't tell me you didn't sense something, because I know you did."

I pause, before realizing that there's no point

arguing with him.

"That wall, actually," I admit, as I watch the video feed. "It's crazy, but I felt like someone was standing there and watching me. I felt the same thing in other parts of the church, but that wall is definitely where I felt it the most." I feel a shiver pass across my shoulders as I realize that I seem to be starting to believe all this crap. "I dunno," I add, "it might have been nothing."

"No, I think I felt the same thing," he mutters, as he takes a couple of items from his pocket and sets them on the ground. "Can you drive the truck very slowly in that direction? Be ready to stop as soon as I tell you."

I start driving the truck along the corridor, but I can't help glancing at the items that he just removed from his pocket. One of them is a vial, just like the vial he was holding earlier in the church.

"So is that really holy water?" I ask.

"Hmm?" He looks at the vial for a moment, before turning back to the monitor. "Yes, it is. Just for protection. Just in case."

"What makes it holy?"

"It's been blessed."

"By who?"

"By me, Mark. Now focus on what we're doing."

I continue to drive the truck along the corridor, but again I glance at the vial.

"So how's it different?" I ask.

"I told you, it's been -"

"Yeah, but what does that change?"

"It means that the water can be used as a sacramental. The exact role and nature of holy water changes from one religion to the next, but it's used in Catholicism, Buddhism, Islam and many others."

"And you're Catholic, right?"

"I'm lots of things, Mark," he replies, still watching the screen. "Keep going."

"How can you be lots of religions at once?"

"I simply meant that I incorporate elements from various practices," he continues, sounding a little annoyed. "That's my job. I have to consider all possibilities, from all faiths. Believe me, it's a tricky situation."

"So this holy water, is it -"

"Stop the truck."

I do as I'm told, but when I look at the screen I still don't see anything other than the bare wall.

"Can any water be holy water?" I ask.

"Any water can be blessed, yes."

"What about pee?"

He scowls at me.

"That's mostly water, right?" I point out. "I'm not trying to be funny! It's a genuine question!"

"You can't bless urine, Mark."

"But can you bless the part of it that *is* water?"

"I'm not having this discussion with you right now."

"But basically any water can be turned into holy water?"

"Yes, but -"

"Just because a priest say that's what it is?"

"Anyone with faith can perform the blessing," he explains, although he sounds a little annoyed. "Now, instead of peppering me with questions, perhaps we can get on with the task at hand?"

He looks back at the screen.

"So this holy water," I continue. "Is it... I mean, what's it used for?"

"A variety of purposes."

"Why did you have some with you yesterday?"

He looks over at me.

"There are certain entities," he says cautiously, "that are deterred by holy water."

"Ghosts are scared of it?"

"No."

"Then why did you have it?" I look at his wrist, where there are still some burn marks. Or at least, they *look* like burn marks. "Did the ghost of that woman attack you?" I pause for a moment, as I think back to when we were in the church earlier.

"Did the ghost of Judith Whatshername make those marks on your arm?"

"Move the truck forward a little."

I push the little joystick, and the truck starts to once more trundle along.

"Slower," Liam says.

"It won't go any slower."

He sighs.

"What else can holy water do?" I ask. "Is it like -"

"I'm not talking any more about holy water!" he snaps. "I brought you along because I thought you might be useful, but if you keep -"

Suddenly he freezes, as he stares at the screen.

"Stop the truck!" he shouts.

"Why?"

"Just stop the damn truck!"

I do what I'm told, but when I look at the screen I still don't see anything except the wall. I don't feel as if I'm being watched, but that might be because I'm viewing the church's interior through the camera that Liam installed on the truck before it was sent inside. As I continue to stare at the screen, however, I notice that the video feed is starting to flicker slightly.

"I saw her," Liam says suddenly.

I turn to him.

"She was there," he continues, and now he

looks white as a sheet, as if he's genuinely shocked by something. "It was only for a frame or two, but I saw her."

"Show me," I reply.

He pauses, and then he swallows hard before closing the laptop's lid.

"Later," he says, getting to his feet. He seems almost to be panicking. "I need to review the images first."

"But can't I at least see the -"

"Later, Mark!" he says firmly. "Can you just stop asking me all these questions? I need to think!"

"Is it the -"

"I have to go back and study this," he continues, turning and hurrying away as I stand up. "I have to compare it."

"What are you talking about?" I call after him, but he's already pushing his way through the overgrown grass, leaving me standing all alone next to the church's door. "What about the little truck?" I shout. "Are we just leaving that in there? Liam? What about the truck?"

***

A few hours later, as the evening sky begins to darken, I'm sitting outside the pub while I wait for Liam. I followed him here from the cemetery, and he told me to sit right here and he said he'd come down to talk to me soon. That was ages ago, though, and I'm starting to think that he's forgotten.

Realizing that this is ridiculous, I get to my feet. I must have been here for two hours now, just doing nothing, and I'm cold. I look up at Liam's window and see that the light is still on, and then I turn to leave.

"There you are," a voice says, and I glance back to see that Liam is finally back down. "I'm sorry I took so long, Mark," he adds, and it's clear that he's pretty flustered by something. "I just..."

His voice trails off for a moment, as if he's lost in thought.

"What are you doing tomorrow morning?" he asks finally.

"Nothing," I reply. "Why? What's going on?"

"I want you to come with me somewhere," he continues. "Will you do that?"

"Where are we going?"

"You'll see. It's not far, just a short drive."

"Can't you at least tell me where -"

"Meet me right here at 8am. Please, Mark. I need you for this."

I want to ask him more questions, but somehow I get the feeling that I'm not going to get any answers. He seems absolutely wrapped up in his thoughts, as if he's barely aware that I'm here. Frankly, he seems more and more crazy with each passing second, but I can't shake the feeling that maybe there's some truth to what he's saying. Or, at least, that I want to find out more.

"I'll be here," I tell him finally, "but can you at least tell me where we're going?"

Turning to me, he pauses before shaking his head.

"Why not?" I ask.

"Because if I told you," he continues, "you most certainly would refuse to come."

"Why?"

"I'll see you here at eight in the morning," he adds, taking a step back, "and get a good night's sleep, Mark. Tomorrow will be... Well, it'll be difficult. You'll need to be strong. Thank you for everything you've done today."

With that, he turns and heads back inside, leaving me standing all alone outside the pub. I want to go after him, to make him give me some actual answers, but instead I sigh as I turn and start walking away along the darkening street. I still don't know quite what happened today, and I definitely don't know what I believe, but I suppose the only way to learn more is to show up tomorrow and see what Liam wants. I have to admit, he gave me the chills just now when he said that tomorrow will be difficult, but that's probably just him being dramatic. I'm sure it'll be fine.

Reaching the cottage, I open the door and

step inside. I want to go to my room and think about things, but as I pass the living room door I stop and see that Caroline and Brian are standing waiting for me.

"We need to talk," Caroline says bitterly, with angry tears in her eyes. "Now!"

CHAPTER SIXTEEN
MARK

"THESE ARE MY PARENTS," Caroline says as she hands me one of the framed photos from the mantelpiece. "Matthew and Laura Neill. They lived here in Briarwych all their lives."

"Okay," I reply tentatively as I look at the picture, "but what -"

"And these are my grandparents," she adds, handing me another picture that looks even older. "They're my father's parents, Anthony and Annie. They also lived here their whole lives, except for the period when my grandfather was serving in the Second World War."

"Cool, but -"

"And here's Anthony with his parents," she says, handing me yet another picture, "Tom and

Peggy, along with Anthony's little brother Jack who died when he was very young. They all lived here in Briarwych their whole lives too."

"That's great," I tell her, "but why -"

"People in Briarwych stick together," she continues, interrupting me again. "Families tend to stay in the area. You knock on any other door, and most people here will be able to tell you the same thing. They'll show you photos of their families going back generations. We don't get many new arrivals, and not many people leave. That means that people here know the village very well. We know what works and what doesn't. And we don't appreciate it when people come to Briarwych and tell us how to live our lives."

"We heard you've spent the day with that priest," Brian says dourly. "What's his name again? Dermott?"

"I was only -"

"I told you to keep away from him," Caroline adds.

"Actually, I don't think you technically said that," I point out.

"Don't be smart!" Brian snaps.

"I'm sure he filled your head with a lot of nonsense about the church," Caroline continues, as she comes over and sits next to me on the sofa. "The truth, the only truth you need to understand, is that nothing needs to be done. That church has stood locked for seventy years now, and it can stand locked for another seventy, for another seven hundred, without anything happening. We've managed to prove that everything will be fine just so long as the door remains locked and nobody goes interfering with the place."

"What do you think is in there?" I ask.

"I honestly don't know."

"But if -"

"And I don't *need* to know," she adds, with fresh tears in her eyes. "Truly, Mark, none of us has any need to know exactly what's in the church. So long as the door stays locked and shut, the situation is contained. And so long as the situation is contained, nobody needs to worry about anything. Do you understand? Everything's fine as it is and it'll continue to be fine. That man wants to interfere, but he's only going to cause trouble. Nobody has been hurt by the church while we've been keeping it contained. We know what's best for Briarwych, not some man who's been sent here by people who don't understand how life works here."

"He only wants to help," I reply, and I'm surprised to realize that I'm defending Liam. "He wants to -"

"He doesn't get it," Brian says.

"He seems to know a lot about the church," I tell him.

"He might have read a lot," he replies, "but

he doesn't know. Not really. And we're the ones who'll have to live with the consequences of his meddling."

"So you'd rather just leave it alone?" I ask, struggling to believe what I'm hearing. "You believe there's something in that church, don't you? Even if you don't know what it is, you believe Judith Prendergast is -"

"Don't say that name!" Caroline snaps angrily.

"But -"

"*Never* say that name! Not in my house! Not in this village!"

As she speaks, she makes the sign of the cross against her chest.

"But you believe something's in there," I continue, "and you just want it left there?"

"We want it to leave us all alone," Brian says, "and so far, our way has worked pretty well. For more than seventy years, no-one got hurt. We left the church alone, and it left us alone in return. You and this Liam Dermott man might not agree with that, but I don't care. It's not your decision to make."

"And what if it's getting stronger?" I ask.

Caroline shakes her head.

"What if it can't be contained forever?" I continue. "What if it's going to find a way out of there?"

"Why would it do that?" Brian replies. "If it's a ghost, it'll just be happy to haunt the place. If it was going to cause any more trouble than that, outside the church, it would've done it by now."

Sighing, I get to my feet and head to the door.

"You're not to speak to that man again," Caroline says. "Do you understand?"

I turn to her.

"I forbid it," she continues. "We both do."

I look over at Brian, hoping for some help.

"You heard what my wife said," he tells me. "Best listen to her, boy."

"This village has managed the church for decades," Caroline continues, "and no-one got hurt. We can do the same again, so long as nobody from outside interferes."

"But somebody *did* get hurt," I remind her. "Kerry got hurt. Kerry died."

"Kerry suffered an aneurysm," she says firmly.

"You know that's not true."

"It's what the autopsy said."

"The autopsy also said that the cause of the aneurysm seemed to be an unnatural swelling of the -"

"That's nonsense."

"Why are you lying?" I ask.

"Language, Mark," she replies, and I can tell

that she's struggling to hold back. "Besides, Kerry had no right going into that church. If anything happened to her in there, she brought it on herself."

"What about the next Kerry who comes along?" I ask.

"Nothing like that will ever happen again."

"You can't be sure of that."

"We'll start by making sure no more outsiders come and cause trouble," she replies, fixing me with a determined stare. "We thought it would be okay to let some people in. That was a mistake. We were wrong."

"In other words," I reply, "you wish you'd never let us come here."

"Kerry would be alive," she says coldly. "The door would never have been breached. That man wouldn't have come to cause trouble."

Brian puts a hand on her shoulder, as if he senses that she's getting angrier.

"I'm sorry we spoiled your perfect village," I tell her, "but it's not our fault. If you leave that church the way it is, sooner or later someone's always going to wander along and get curious. It's just human nature. That church is like a landmine, waiting for someone to step on it. You can try to leave it alone and cover it up, but someone'll stumble onto it eventually."

"Not if they mind their own business."

"Bullshit!" I blurt out, although I

178

immediately know that I've said too much.

"Go to your room, Mark," Caroline replies. "Perhaps you can spend some time thinking about your behavior. And I hope you understand that you are under no circumstances to have any contact with Liam Dermott again. If you so much as mention his name, we'll have no choice but to send you straight back to London. Is that what you want? To live in a filthy, crime-ridden hell?"

"London's not that bad," I tell her.

"Go to your room. And don't answer back."

Sighing, I turn and head out into the hallway, and then I make my way up the stairs. I want to punch something, but somehow I manage to hold my temper. By the time I get up onto the landing, however, I already know exactly where I'll be at 8am tomorrow morning.

AMY CROSS

CHAPTER SEVENTEEN
MARK

"I WASN'T SURE THAT you'd come," Liam says, his breath visible in the air as he leads me over to his car in the street outside the pub. "I thought maybe yesterday's excitement might have scared you off."

"I'm not scared off by anything," I reply. "Especially people who make threats."

"Threats?"

"Never mind."

"We're just taking a short trip to Crenford," he explains, before unlocking the car and climbing inside. "I don't know whether you know the place, but it's not too far away."

I climb into the passenger seat.

"What are we gonna do there?" I ask.

"I'll explain once we've arrived."

"Why can't you explain now?"

"Because, frankly, I'm worried you'd get right out of this car and refuse to come with me." He pauses. "I actually *need* your help, Mark," he adds, as he starts the engine. "This would be a little difficult without you."

I wait as he eases the car away from the parking spot, and then I sit in silence as he drives along the street. We take the next turn, and I glance out at the Neills' cottage as we go past. There's a light on in the living room, which means Caroline and Brian must be out of bed now. I guess they've probably looked in my room, which means they must know I've snuck out. Which means my fate is sealed and they'll be sending me back to London as soon as they can.

So much for a fresh start in Briarwych. This whole visit has turned out to be a complete dead-end.

***

"So what does Judith Prendergast want?" I ask as I follow Liam away from the car, toward a large, nondescript building over by the gate. "I mean, do ghosts actually want something, or are they just happy floating about and scaring people?"

"Contrary to popular belief," he replies, as

he checks his watch, "ghosts don't spend their time banging chains or slamming doors. Not *real* ghosts, anyway. They tend to remain because of some unfinished business, and this usually becomes something of an obsession with them."

"So what's Judith Prendergast obsessed about?"

"I have a few theories, but I'm not quite certain yet."

"If she didn't like Kerry and me going into the church," I continue, "then why did she unlock the door in the first place?"

"I've been wondering the same thing myself."

"Why did she let us in, and then kill Kerry?"

"That's one of the big questions that's bothering me," he says as we reach a door and he swipes a card. The door clicks and he pulls it open. "There's another one that's causing me even more trouble, however."

"What's that?"

"I'm not just wondering why she killed Kerry," he says, turning to me. "I'm also wondering why she let *you* live."

"Oh." I pause for a moment. "I didn't think about it like that."

"Maybe it's just that Kerry was loud and blasphemous. After all, you *did* tell me that she sat on the altar." He pauses. "Or maybe it's something else. I think it's something else. Come on, let's get this over with."

"Get what over with?" I ask as he heads inside. Before I can follow, I spot a blue and white sign on the wall, and I feel a shiver pass through my chest as I realize where we are. "Crenford Coroner's Office?" I say cautiously. "Why are we at Crenford Coroner's Office?"

***

"I told you this was going to be difficult," Liam says, keeping his voice low as we stand in an empty, brightly-lit corridor. "I wish I could tell you that it's okay to back out, but the truth is that I need you here. You're my only link to her."

"I don't want to see Kerry's body," I tell him, struggling to hold back tears. "Why didn't you say we were coming here?"

"Because you'd have refused."

"Damn straight!"

"I arranged for her burial to be postponed," he explains. "It's not as if she had any family-members who were trying to make arrangements. I was hoping I wouldn't need to come here and do this, but I'm afraid I need to know exactly what Kerry went through when she was in the church that night. I need to know exactly who or what she encountered."

"I told you, she -"

"I need to know her side of it."

"Good luck with that," I reply, "because she's dead."

"That's where you come in," he says. "She's been gone for a little over two weeks. That means that there's still time to speak to her."

"What the fuck are you talking about?" I ask.

"I can bring her back, for a few minutes," he tells me. "I don't expect you to believe me right now, but you'll see the proof for yourself in a moment or two. I could maybe do it alone, but you knew her, you were with her when she died. Your presence will make the process far easier." He pauses, watching me as if he expects me to suddenly just agree with him. "I know you're scared, but -"

"I'm not scared!" I snap.

"Really? I would be, in your position." He pauses again. "I need you to battle through the fear, Mark, instead of pretending that it isn't there. I wouldn't ask you to bear witness to this today, if I didn't absolutely need you. I was up all night researching some very old texts, and I believe that your friend is in a position to confirm or refute my theory about what's really happening at Briarwych Church. There's no -"

Before he can finish, a nearby door creaks

open and a man emerges from one of the rooms, wearing a white uniform.

"She's ready," he says softly.

"It's time," Liam tells me. "I'm begging you, find the strength to come and do this. You have no idea how important it could be. Not just for Briarwych, but for the whole world."

I take a deep breath, determined to tell him that I'm out of here, but as I look at the open door I can't help wondering whether Kerry's body is really in the next room. I don't want to see her, of course; I mean, who *would*? At the same time, I've come this far and I feel like she should get some justice, and right now Liam seems to be the only person who actually gives a damn about what happened to her. If all of this had been left up to Caroline and Brian and the others in Briarwych, Kerry would probably have been buried by now and nobody would be asking any more questions.

"Okay," I say finally, although my voice is trembling slightly. "Let's get it over with, yeah?"

"Thank you."

He heads over to the door, where he stops and whispers something to the technician. Then he goes into the next room, leaving me to take another deep breath before I start to follow. With each step I feel more and more anxious, until I reach the door and I swear my chest is going to crush in on itself. As the technician steps aside and then walks away, I stop in the doorway and freeze as I see the pale, lifeless body on a metal table in the center of the examination room.

It's her.

Somehow, I was hoping it wouldn't be Kerry, that this would all turn out to be some kind of sick mistake. Even from here, however, I can see the side of her face and can tell that it's definitely her.

I want to be sick, but instead I step into the room. At least there's no stench, and the whole scene feels strangely calm. They've even put a gray sheet over her torso and upper legs, to give her some dignity, although as I step closer I can see that there are two thick jagged lines running up from beneath the sheet and almost to her shoulders, with stitches holding the edges of her skin together. I guess that must be a wound that's left over from the autopsy.

For a moment, I can't help but imagine her brain being removed and weighed, and all her guts too. They must have been poking around inside her for hours, trying to figure out why she died.

"Are you okay?" Liam asks.

I nod.

"If you're not, you can -"

"I'm fine," I say firmly. "Just leave it, okay?"

I can't stop looking at Kerry's face, however.

Last time I saw her, in the kitchen at the Neills' cottage, she looked like she was in pain, but at least there was some color to her skin. Now she looks completely calm, but she's totally white as well. I guess they took all her blood out before they put her in the freezer.

Turning, I see that Liam's setting out some items on a nearby trolley. I spot another vial of holy water, which seems to be something he carries wherever he goes, as well as various small trinkets and jewels.

"Two weeks isn't an inordinately long time," he explains. "It shouldn't take too long at all to bring her back."

"This is nuts," I tell him. "You'd better not disrespect her."

"I would never do that," he says, as he takes a small bottle from his pocket and unscrews the lid. "This entire procedure is about finding out what really happened to her. I think that's pretty respectful. Don't you?"

I don't answer. Instead, I just stare down at Kerry's face. I want to apologize to her, to tell her that I'm sorry I didn't stop her going into the church. I know it's not really my fault, but I still feel like I could have done something different. A moment later, noticing something flickering nearby, I turn to see that Liam has lit two small candles, which he proceeds to place on either side of Kerry's head.

"What are those for?" I ask.

"Even the dead need a little warmth," he replies calmly. "We have to provide all the encouragement that we can, to get her soul back here."

"Back from where?"

"That's the sixty-four million dollar question, isn't it?" He lights two more candles and then places them on either side of her neck, just above her shoulders. "I always maintain that it's best we don't know too much about the world beyond this one. Otherwise, we might not treat this life with the reverence that it requires."

He lights another pair of candles and then walks around the table, before setting them down next to Kerry's feet.

"But this isn't actually gonna work, is it?" I ask. "What are you gonna do? Are you gonna pretend she's talking through you, something like that?"

He doesn't respond. Instead, he takes a vial of holy water and unscrews the lid, and then he carefully sprinkles some drops on Kerry's forehead. They quickly start dribbling down onto her eyes and then down the sides of her cheeks, like tears.

"Are you sure you should be doing that?" I ask.

He empties the rest of the vial onto Kerry's neck and shoulders, before putting the vial away and then taking a small wooden cross and gently setting it on Kerry's forehead.

"How do you know this shit works?" I continue. "Have you done it before?"

"I have assisted before."

"And what happened?"

"In some of the cases, absolutely nothing. In others, we succeeded in bringing the subject back for a short time. Father Merrisford taught me what I know when it comes to these techniques, he was very well-versed in the scriptures and he had a certain knack when it came to the darker arts." He takes a small book from his pocket and begins to search through its pages. "It might take a while," he adds, "to stir her from her rest. A lot depends on what happened to her soul after death. She might be too far away to..."

His voice trails off, and he glances at me.

"Well," he adds, "let's hope for the best. This might be boring for you, but please stay in the room."

Once he's found whatever he was looking for in the book, he sets it down before taking a small knife and pressing the blade against his finger. I'm about to ask him what he's doing, but suddenly he slices the blade and a bead of blood runs from the wound.

"This is getting weirder," I tell him.

Ignoring me, he reaches down with his other

hand and touches Kerry's left eyelid. I want to tell him to stop, but instead I wince as I watch him opening the lid to reveal Kerry's dead, marble-like left eye. And then, tilting his other hand, Liam waits until the dribble of blood falls and lands directly on Kerry's eyeball.

"Man, you shouldn't be doing this," I say through gritted teeth, as I watch the blood trickle to the corner of her eyes. "Come on, none of this is actually going to do anything, is it? It's just bullshit."

He picks the book back up and looks at the pages for a moment. And then, before I can ask what the book's about, he starts reading in some weird language that I don't understand. Maybe it's Latin or Greek or some stuff like that, but he's keeping his voice low as he talks and I feel like maybe I shouldn't interrupt him.

Looking down at Kerry's face again, I watch her eyes. One is still closed, and the other remains open with the trickle of blood having run down to the corner next to the bridge of her nose. I stare for a moment, before realizing that this is dumb and that I don't even know what I'm waiting for. It's not like she's going to suddenly sit up and start talking, but I guess Liam has managed to sucker me with all his talk about bringing people back, and with all these stupid props he's brought along. Seriously, I can't even believe that he was able to get permission to do something like this.

Finally, feeling a little sick, I turn and head over to the window. The blinds are closed, and when I open them a little I see nothing more than a boring old car park. The sky looks pretty dark in the distance, so I guess there might be rain later. There's nothing particularly interesting about the view, but at least it's better than looking at Kerry's dead body. This whole trip is completely pointless and it's a colossal waste of our time. As Liam continues to read, I watch the car park in the hope that something interesting might happen out there, and then I let out a sigh.

Liam's a liar. This whole thing is pointless.

CHAPTER EIGHTEEN
MARK

WITH MY EYES STILL closed, I sit on the floor with my back to the wall and try to ignore the sound of Liam's voice droning on and on. He's been reading from that book for almost two hours now, and I'm starting to think that the guy really doesn't know when to give up. He might know a lot of useful information about churches and religions and shit like that, but I think he's really overreaching himself with this crazy ritual he's performing.

He's also driving me nuts.

Opening my eyes, I look over at the table and see that nothing has changed. Liam's still reading from that book, and Kerry's body is still flat on its back with the sheet covering all but her head, shoulders and feet. The candles are still burning, and I suppose the blood's still in her eye, but nothing's actually happening. And as my frustration continues to grow, I finally get to my feet and check my pockets for a few coins.

"I'm going to check out that vending machine," I tell Liam, before heading to the door. "I'll be back in a minute or two."

Instead of replying, he simply continues to read from the book. I sigh as I push the door open, and then I make my way along the corridor until I reach the machine at the far end. I was hoping to get a Coke, but I don't have enough coins so I have to make do with a shitty carton of orange juice. As I slide the coins one-by-one into the slot, I remind myself that I'm in no hurry to get back into the other room. I don't know how long Liam intends to keep going with all this rubbish, but I feel like I'm about to lose my temper. Honestly, I'm having to hold back from punching this stupid machine.

"Fuck!" I mutter, as I put the last coin in and then close my eyes, leaning my head for a moment against the glass panel as I hear the machine slowly starting to spit out the carton.

I'm trying to keep my shit together, but I can still just about hear Liam's voice drifting through from the main room and I just want to tell him to shut the hell up. Lately I've been getting pretty good at controlling my anger, but right now he's pushing me like I've never been pushed before and a moment later I realize I've inadvertently closed both my hands to form fists. I hear the carton dropping into the tray at the bottom of the machine, but all I can focus on is the fact that this sense of anger is growing and growing in my body. It's almost like I'm panicking, and finally I realize this has all gone on long enough.

"No more," I whisper, before opening my eyes and storming back along the corridor, breaking into a run as I reach the door and hurry back into the next room. "Stop!" I shout at Liam. "You have to stop right now! This isn't working!"

I wait, shaking with rage, but he's still calmly reading from that stupid book.

"Why won't you stop?" I yell, and then I hurry over and reach out to snatch the book from his hands. "Just stop already! You're gonna -"

Suddenly he stops, and at that moment I feel a powerful presence rush against my body. I immediately look down, and I see with a sense of horror that both of Kerry's eyes are now wide open, and she's staring straight up at me.

CHAPTER NINETEEN
KERRY

I WANT THIS FEELING to go away right now. This is exactly how it was, just before the ambulance crew got to me, when I was seconds from dying.

"Um," I manage to say finally, as I start shivering violently, "I think I..."

I pause, and then suddenly everything goes black and I feel myself slump down to the floor.

And then I open my eyes and see Mark standing right above me, staring down at me with a gormless, stupid look on his face. I immediately try to open my mouth to tell him to go away, but somehow I can't get my mouth to open, and then I realize that the ceiling looks different. It's as if I'm not in the Neills' stupid little cottage anymore. This ceiling looks more like something you'd see in a hospital, but that doesn't make sense unless somehow I collapsed and now I'm waking up.

Did I collapse?

Suddenly a second face appears. A man leans over me, and he looks troubled by something.

"Fuck," Mark says, before stepping back out of my field of vision. "Fuck, fuck, fuck, this is some kind of -"

"Don't go," the man replies, cutting him off. "Mark, you have to stay. Your presence is important."

I try again to speak, to ask them what's wrong, but I'm really struggling to move my mouth. After a moment I manage to feel my jaw again, and I feel my lips parting slightly, but the effort is really crazy and I'm struggling to keep from panicking. I remember a guy I used to know, Mr. Abercrombie from the flat opposite, and he had a stroke one time and he ended up in a wheelchair and he could hardly move one side of his face. I'm way too young for that to have happened to me, but I can't help feeling a growing sense of panic.

Why can't I move my body properly?

"Mark, stay," the man says, looking away from me for a moment, as if he's staring at Mark across the room. "We've come this far. We have to stay the course now."

I try to turn and look at Mark, but I can't

move my head. I can't blink, either, and I'm starting to realize that I feel really, *really* wrong. And still. I feel as if nothing's moving anywhere in my body. I never really noticed before, but I always used to have a sense of my own heartbeat; it was something I took for granted, something I didn't really notice until it was gone. Why can't I feel my own heart beating? And why am I so fucking cold?

"Kerry," the man says as he looks back down at me, "my name is Father Liam Dermott. Can you hear me?"

When I try to speak, I feel my mouth open a little more, but I still can't actually get any words out.

"I'm going to take that as a yes," he continues. "It'll take a moment before you're able to properly respond, that's completely normal in a situation where the body has..."

His voice trails off for a few seconds.

"Well, let's just say that it's understandable," he adds. "Kerry, we probably only have a few minutes, so I'm afraid I'm going to have to press you on this, and you're going to have to do your absolute best to answer. I'm so sorry I can't do more for you, but you have to understand that I wouldn't have brought you back unless it was absolutely necessary."

As he says those words, Mark slowly leans back into my view. He's staring down at me with that same shocked expression on his face. I want to punch him, but at the same time this sense of panic is growing and growing as I try to work out why I'm so cold.

"That night in the church," the Liam guy continues, "you saw something, didn't you? I need to know exactly what it looked like, and what it said to you."

I try again to get my mouth open, and this time it's a little easier. When I try to speak, however, all that emerges from my throat is a faint, guttural groan.

"Kerry, it's okay!" Mark stammers. "You're -"

"Quiet!" Liam snaps at him. "Don't tell her! She won't be able to handle it!"

"What happened to me?" I manage to whimper, as I try desperately to move my hands, or my feet, or any other part of my body at all.

"I need you to focus, Kerry," Liam continues, leaning closer to my face. "That night in the church, what exactly did you see? Did it look like a woman, or did it look like something else? This is important, Kerry. I need you to think back to that night."

"Where am I?" I ask, finally managing to turn my head a little so that I can look directly at Mark. "Why am I here?"

"Stay focused," Liam says, touching the

side of my face and gently tilting my head back to face him. I try to resist, but he's too strong and the warmth of his hand is overwhelming. "Tell me what she looked like."

"She looked like a woman," I reply. "Just a woman."

"*This* woman?" he asks, and then he holds up a photo for me to see. "The woman on the left of the back row. Is that the woman you saw in the church?"

"I..."

Struggling to focus, I take a moment to look at the picture. As soon as I see the woman's face, however, I feel a shudder run up through my chest.

"It's her," I say, and now it's getting a little easier to speak. "She was wearing black, and she looked..."

My voice trails off as I stare at the photo.

"Angrier," I add finally. "There was something about her face, a kind of darkness. It was like she hated me, like she was twisted with anger."

For a moment, I think back to the sight of that woman leaning toward me, and then I remember her cold hand on the side of my face. She was speaking to me, asking me over and over to explain why I was in the church. Then when Mark came closer, she started asking him the same thing, until finally he reached out and touched my arm. That was when she leaned right against my ear, and

I felt the coldness of the last words she whispered before she vanished

"Shattak," I stammer.

"What was that?" Liam asks, leaning closer.

"Sattiak," I say again, "or... Santak, something like that. Shattak? I don't know."

I remember my heart was pounding.

"Why am I so cold?" I whimper, as I feel my eyes swelling with the coming of tears. Except, there *are* no tears. "What's wrong with me? Why can't I sit up?"

"Shaltak," Liam says firmly. "Is that what she said to you, Kerry?"

"Yes. Maybe. I think so. But why can't I move?"

"Are you sure? Try to think back. Did she say the name Shaltak?"

"Mark, what's happening?" I ask, turning to him again. I can feel my bottom lip trembling. "What are they doing to me?"

I wait, but he's staring at me with tears in his eyes and I'm starting to feel really scared.

"Please," I continue, trying to reach out to him but not quite managing to move my hands. "I don't remember what happened after I was in the kitchen. Am I in a hospital? Why am I here? What happened to me?"

"Do something!" Mark hisses, looking across me toward Liam. "Help her!"

"There's nothing I *can* do," he replies. "I'm so sorry."

"But she'll get better, right?" he continues. "You've brought her back from the dead and now she's going to recover. Right?"

"This is only a temporary reprieve," he explains. "Nothing more."

"What are you talking about?" I ask. "Who did you bring back from the dead? Who's dead?"

I can feel myself starting to panic. And with each second of silence that passes as I wait for an answer, I can tell that the panic is growing and growing.

"Who's dead?" I ask again. "Why are you both looking at me like that?"

"You have to help her!" Mark snaps. "You brought her back, so why can't you let her stay?"

"It doesn't work like that," Liam replies.

"You can't let her die again!"

"She's still dead, Mark!" he says firmly, before turning to look down at me again. "This is just a brief reprieve. I was able to draw her soul back to her body, but soon she'll be gone and this time it'll be permanent." He pauses, with tears in his eyes. "I'm so sorry, Kerry," he adds, "but there's really, truly nothing I can do. You have to go back.

"Back where?" I stammer, still trying again and again to sit up. I think I can just about feel my body now, but everything's so cold. "Where are you taking me?"

"It's okay," Mark says, leaning closer, "I won't let anything happen to you, not again. We're going to find a way to keep you here. We're not going to lose you again."

"What do you mean, *lose* me?" I ask, although now I'm starting to find it harder to speak. "What's happening to me? Why are you talking to me like this?"

"You died, Kerry," Mark continues. "You died two weeks ago, but Liam brought you back to life and now we're going to save you. I don't care what anyone says, we're going to -"

"Don't make promises you can't keep," Liam tells him.

"We *are* going to keep it!" he shouts, turning to him as they both lean over me. "How can you say you can't save her, when you've already brought her back from the dead?"

"I'm not dead!" I stammer, but I'm starting to feel even colder than before. "How can I be dead? I'm right here!"

"You'll go back to wherever you went after you died," Liam says, clearly struggling to stay calm. "It's that simple, Kerry."

"I haven't been anywhere!" I sob. "Why are you saying these things?"

"Wherever you were between your death and this moment, you'll return and -"

"There was nothing!" I scream, struggling harder than ever in a desperate attempt to rise up from wherever I am right now. "I haven't been anywhere! I was in the kitchen and then I was here! There wasn't anywhere else!"

"Is that true?" Mark asks, looking over at Liam again. "Where do people go when they die?"

"I didn't go anywhere!" I whimper. "It's like I was asleep, but without any dreams! It was just nothing! Please, you can't make me go back to that! It wasn't real! It can't have been real, I can't have been dead!"

"I'm so sorry, Kerry," Liam says. "I would never have brought you back at all, if I hadn't needed to ask you about that night in the church."

"He's lying!" I shout, turning to Mark again. "Please, Mark, tell me it's all a lie. I can't be dead. There was nothing between being in the kitchen and being here. It was just black and cold, it's like I didn't exist. Please don't let me go back to that. Please find a way to keep me here."

"She's weakening," Liam says.

"No, I'm not!" I shout, but in that instant I can already feel myself slipping into darkness. "Don't make me go back to how I was! There wasn't anything there! I didn't exist!"

"We're going to find a way," Mark says. "I swear to you, no matter what it takes, we'll find a way to keep you here."

"I'm so sorry," Liam tells me. "There's nothing I can do."

"I don't want to go back to nothing!" I reply, but I'm slurring my words now and I can barely move my mouth. "Please, I'm so cold and I'm scared. You can't make me go back, you have to find a way to let me -"

Suddenly I feel myself falling, and my vision starts to fade. It's the same feeling I remember from before, from the night I was stabbed and from the moment just before I collapsed in the kitchen. This time, however, I can't figure out how to fight back, but my senses are starting to fade and I realize I've only got a few seconds. I can hear Mark and Liam still talking, still arguing, but I can barely make out their voices. The cold is fading, but so is the sensation of having a body at all.

I'm so terrified, all I can do is scream, and then everything goes black.

CHAPTER TWENTY
MARK

RAIN IS FALLING MORE steadily now, starting to tap constantly against the windshield as we sit in Liam's car. We haven't spoken for a while now, not since we came back out to the car park, and in my mind I'm just replaying that final scream over and over again. She sounded terrified, and then suddenly the scream just ended.

Finally, I turn and see that Liam is staring straight ahead.

"Where is she now?" I ask.

He glances at me.

"She said there was nothing," I continue, "but that can't be right, can it? I mean, *you* don't believe that there's nothing, do you?"

"Mark..."

"What about ghosts?" I add. "If ghosts are real, then there's something after death."

"Ghosts are the souls of people who've refused to pass from this world," he replies. "Those who *do* pass simply... go. There's no revolving door, Mark. Once a soul leaves, it can't come back."

"But you just brought Elizabeth back!" I point out.

"I temporarily raised her from what's left of her body," he explains. "It's not like I opened a door and brought her back from somewhere. I simply created the correct circumstances that would allow her to exist again for a few minutes."

"You don't believe her, though, do you?" I ask. "You're a priest. You have to believe that there's something that comes after death."

I wait, but he doesn't reply. Instead, he seems lost in his own thoughts, as if he's still trying to deal with the way Kerry screamed as she died. The scream was suddenly cut off, as if Kerry simply stopped existing, as if she was there one moment and gone the next.

"So where is she now?" I add.

"We have to get back to Briarwych," he says, suddenly reaching out and starting the engine. "There's no time to lose. I have to begin the process of cleansing the church immediately."

"You mean getting rid of the ghost?"

"I told them containment wouldn't work," he

continues, already backing the car out of the parking bay. "Maybe it would have done, if what we were dealing with had been *just* a ghost. But it's not, Mark. That thing in Briarwych Church is far more than just the ghost of Judith Prendergast."

"What do you mean?" I ask. "She died and now she's a ghost. Isn't that all there is to it?"

"I need to check one more thing before I'm sure," he replies, "but I think I'm finally starting to understand what happened in that church all those years ago, before Judith Prendergast died."

***

As the car comes to a halt outside the pub in Briarwych, I can't shake a feeling of dread in my gut. Liam was mostly quiet on the drive back here, only responding very briefly to my attempts to ask him questions. It's clear that his conversation with Kerry left him even more concerned than before, and as I glance out the window and spot the church's spire I can't shake the feeling that I still don't really understand what's happening here in this village.

"I need you to come inside with me and help carry some equipment," Liam says after a moment.

"Where to?" I ask, turning to him.

Please don't be the church.

"To the church," he says, and I can hear the

fear in his voice. "I'm going to need your help with a few things, Mark. I wouldn't ask you, but it's vital. I can't do this alone."

"But -"

"And you're the best person for the job."

"Me?" Shocked, I wait for him to admit that he's joking. "I'm not really good at anything," I add finally, trying to think of a way out of this mess. "I'm just an idiot, I'm not very good at helping anyone."

"You pick up on things," he replies.

"I don't pick up on anything!"

"I've noticed it over the past couple of days," he says. "Despite your protestations, you sense the evil in that church, don't you?"

"I..."

My voice trails off as I think back to the feeling of being watched.

"It's okay," he continues, "there's no need to be scared. Everyone has a different degree of awareness. Some don't pick up on anything. Others pick up on just enough to know that they should be cautious. Others pick up on a lot more. Some even see and hear things." He watches me closely. "Have you ever seen or heard anything, Mark?" he asks finally. "Voices, perhaps?"

"No," I reply, although I can already hear the defensiveness in my own voice. "I mean, not really. I mean... Not in the church."

"Where?"

"Maybe at that old airfield," I continue. "I don't know, it might have been nothing, but I think I heard a voice."

"What was the voice saying?"

"It was begging for a priest," I tell him. "I think it was coming from an old bed, but there was no-one on the bed. It might have been a joke, though. It might have been someone pranking me for a TV show or a YouTube channel."

"That airfield was used for experimental planes during the war," he replies. "There were plenty of accidents out there. Men died."

"That doesn't mean I heard anything."

"But you did."

Sighing, I try to figure out why he's wrong, but I can't.

"You have a sensitivity to these things that's quite rare," he continues, "and that, unfortunately, makes you perfect for helping me today. I'll keep you safe, I promise. I know how to perform this ceremony, so it's just a matter of getting it done. The hardest part will be staying calm, but I can't afford to wait days for someone else to arrive and assist me." He pauses, as rain continues to patter against the roof of the car. "The fact that your sensitivity has emerged without guidance, without any kind of training, is very impressive," he adds. "With the right help, you could really make something of it."

"I don't want to," I tell him.

"It won't go away."

"I don't want to be part of this," I add, feeling a rising sense of fear along with an urgent need to get out of this car and never come near Briarwych again. "I didn't ask to get involved."

"Neither did you friend Kerry," he replies, "and you saw her today, dead on that slab. She's never coming back, Mark, not after we spoke to her. And wherever she is now, she's there because of the entity that's infesting Briarwych Church. Forgive me if this seems a little manipulative, but I'm getting desperate. Don't you want to help make that thing pay for what it did to Kerry?"

I pause for a moment, thinking back to the way she begged us to save her.

"How do you still believe in God?" I ask finally.

Turning, I see a flicker of concern on his face.

"After seeing things like that," I continue, "how can you still believe in anything good?"

"You're not the first person who's ever asked me that," he replies.

"So how do you do it?"

"I've seen some terrible things," he replies. "I've seen children dying in the most appalling circumstances. I've seen demons, creatures of pure evil, practicing their dark arts in our world. I watched my own wife die of brain cancer."

"I wouldn't still have faith after that," I tell him. "Not in anything. If you've seen all that bad shit, have you ever seen anything good?"

"My faith doesn't exist *despite* the bad things," he explains, "but *because* of them. I still believe that there's balance to the world, Mark. And whenever I see something truly awful, or truly evil, I firmly believe that somewhere there's an equal powerful force for good. Maybe that force doesn't make itself so readily apparent in our world, maybe it doesn't flaunt itself, but I believe it's out there somewhere. I can only assume that it's waiting for us."

"And that's enough?" I ask. "That keeps you going?"

"That keeps me going," he replies. "What would be the alternative?"

***

As soon as Liam opens the door and steps into the pub, all the talk stops and the place falls silent. Everyone turns to watch us as we enter, and I can't help feeling like I'm in one of those horror films where all the locals suddenly turn against the outsiders.

"Gentlemen," Liam says cautiously, as he

steps into the middle of the room and looks around at all the drinkers. "Ladies."

He looks over at the bar, where his bags have been neatly packed.

"Thank you to whoever brought all of that down from my room," he continues. "You've saved me the trouble of -"

"We think it's time for you to leave now," the barman says, interrupting him. "No offense, but we've been talking and we don't want any more interference. We want to be left alone."

"And then what will happen?" Liam asks.

"Then life will go on as before," another man says.

Liam turns to him. "For how long?"

"For as long as no-one opens that door."

"That's not how it works, I'm afraid," Liam replies. "You don't know what you're dealing with here."

"We know it's stayed in the church for all these years," a woman tells him, her voice shaking with fear. "We know it doesn't bother us, as long as we don't bother it."

"We've all tried to leave," a man adds. "We've all tried to sell up and go, but no-one'll buy here in Briarwych. They come and take a look around, they say how pretty it is, then they leave and we never hear from them again. It's like on some level they sense what's going on. So we've had to accept, all of us, that this is how things have to be."

"I can change that," Liam says. "I can get rid of it."

Spotting my bags over in the corner, I turn and see that Caroline and Brian Neill are standing nearby.

"We've called Mrs. Trevor," Caroline says coldly, staring at me with barely-disguised hatred. "We warned you what would happen if you disobeyed us. She's coming to pick you up tomorrow. Tonight you can stay here at the pub. We don't want you in the house anymore."

"Are you serious?" I ask.

"We should never have had you and the girl come to stay with us," she continues, folding her arms across her chest. "We just wanted to be good people and help out a couple of kids who needed a home. Look how that backfired. We ended up with a a couple of ungrateful little bastards who -"

"Hey!" I snap, stepping toward her.

"Don't make this difficult," Brian says, moving past his wife and standing right in front of me. "I'm sorry it didn't work out, Mark, but you've only got yourself to blame."

"All this," I reply, "because you're scared of a ghost?"

"We can live with that ghost," he says firmly. "What we can't live with is people like you, who interfere."

I open my mouth to tell him that he's a coward, but at the last moment I manage to hold back. There's no point making the situation even worse.

"It's not a ghost," Liam says suddenly.

We both turn to him.

"It's not *just* a ghost, anyway," he continues, as he looks around at all the people gathered here in the pub. "I first became suspicious when I spotted some markings on the wall in the church. Then I spoke to the spirit of Kerry Lawrence today, and she confirmed my worst fears. I don't know exactly how it all started here in Briarwych, I don't know what happened to Judith Prendergast when she was alive, but I'm quite certain now that at the time of her death she had become possessed by the spirit of a demon that goes by the name of Shaltak."

"What are you talking about?" I ask.

"That thing in the church isn't *just* the ghost of Judith Prendergast," he explains. "It's her ghost mixed with Shaltak's presence. That's why it has become so cruel and persistent, and it's why it has been slowly growing in strength over the years. Frankly, I'd have thought that it would have forced its way out of the church by now, but for some reason it has remained cowering in there. That won't last forever, though, so the only option is to perform a ceremony that will cleanse Briarwych Church forever. That's the ceremony I shall be performing this afternoon."

"With all due respect," Tim Murphy says from the bar, "that's not your decision to make."

"I have the necessary authority," Liam replies. "You know that's true. The church doesn't belong to the village, and the responsibility of dealing with its infestation does not fall to any of you. It falls to the authorities that I represent, and I can't afford to wait any longer. So I'm afraid that, whether you like it or not, this madness ends today." Stepping over to the bar area, he picks up a couple of his bags and then turns to me. "Mark, can you help me please?"

I hesitate, before looking over at the Neills and seeing the hatred in their eyes.

"Sure," I mutter, and then I grab the rest of Liam's things and help him carry them to the door.

"You'll bring ruin on this village," Tim Murphy calls after us. "We had everything under control until you showed up, Father Dermott."

Once we're outside, I help carry Liam's things to the car. The rain is getting a little worse now, and when I glance back toward the pub I see that they're all talking again, no doubt discussing everything that just happened. Turning to Liam, I watch as he opens one of his cases and checks the contents.

"What if they try to stop us?" I ask.

"They won't. They'll do what they've always done. They'll go to their homes and they'll draw the curtains and they'll pray that nothing happens. And nothing will happen, at least from their perspectives. Because tomorrow morning their lives will carry on. It'll likely take them quite some time to realize that the evil is gone from Briarwych. They're so accustomed to living in fear, and change won't be easy."

"But was that true?" I ask. "What you said in there, I mean. There's not actually a demon in the church, is there? Demons aren't real."

"I'm afraid they are," he replies. "Maybe ghosts can be ignored, but demons can't." He closes the case and turns to me. "Now, are you going to help me or not?"

CHAPTER TWENTY-ONE
MARK

WITH EVERY STEP THAT we take across the cemetery, the church spire seems to grow taller, until finally we're standing right outside the wooden door and I look up through the rain and see the church towering high above us. From this angle, the spire looks so sharp, it's almost as if it could rip through the sky at any moment.

"Someone should have confronted this thing a long time ago," Liam says as he stops at the door and fumbles for something in his pockets. "If they had, Briarwych wouldn't have spent seventy years living in fear, and your friend would still be alive."

I watch as he loosens the lock, and then finally he opens the door and I feel a shiver pass through my body as I look along the gloomy corridor and see the far wall.

"It's here," I say cautiously. "I can sense it. It's watching us."

"Of course it is," he replies, picking his bags back up and stepping across the threshold, into the church. "It's not stupid. It's cautious, but never believe that these things are stupid."

I know I should follow him, but for a moment I can't quite pluck up the courage. Turning, I look back across the cemetery, but to my surprise there's still nobody else in sight. I really thought that some of the locals would come and try to argue with us again, but it seems Liam was right when he said they'd all keep well away. I guess they're still in the pub, or in their homes, hoping that nothing will happen and that everything will go on as before.

"Are you coming inside?" Liam asks. "We need to get started."

***

"If she knows that we're here," I say a few minutes later, as Liam and I unpack his cases in the office near the rear of the church, "why doesn't she try to stop us?"

"Actually, I've been wondering that myself," he replies. "As demons go, Shaltak seems especially cautious."

"So it's not actually Judith Prendergast?" I

ask.

"It's her," he explains, "but she's still possessed by Shaltak. I don't understand why or how, but I suppose she was possessed at the moment of her death all those years ago, and somehow they're still entwined. I'm sorry, Mark, but I can't go into the exact details because I simply don't know." He looks past me, and I turn to see that he's looking at some scratches at the bottom of the nearest wall. "The entity haunting this church is most likely a kind of amalgamation of Judith and the demon, although the demon is undoubtedly stronger."

"And that mark on the wall proves that there's really a demon here?"

"That's one of the few things you can rely on a demon to do," he replies. "They love hearing and seeing their names. In cases of possession, they always take on the form of their human victim. Not just the form, either. They take on the voice, the expressions, they take on pretty much everything. The one thing a demon really has, of its own, is its name. So they rather childishly enjoy seeing and hearing their names whenever and wherever possible, even if that means -"

Before he can finish, there's a brief, faint shuffling sound out in the corridor. We turn and look, but there's no-one in the doorway and – for once – I don't feel as if we're being watched.

"So if this thing is a demon," I say after a moment, "why doesn't it just kill us and leave the church?"

"It's cautious, for some reason," he replies. "That caution means it prefers to wait and see what we're doing first. I have no idea what can be causing the caution, but -"

Something bumps against a wall out in the corridor.

"She *is* getting more confident, though," he adds. "Seventy years is nothing to a demon."

He sets a book on the table, and I can't help but notice that his hands are shaking slightly. I think he's actually scared.

"So what is a demon?" I ask finally. "You said its name is Shaltak, right?"

He nods.

"So who is Shaltak? What does she want?"

"To be free in the mortal world," he replies. "To cause trouble. They usually have no greater aim than that. They just seek to create chaos and pain and turmoil among mankind, as if they just want to prove that they can. They seem to get some kind of kick out of revealing mankind's every fault and failing. That's why they don't simply kill indiscriminately. They want us to kill each other, to torture each other, so they dedicate their time to making that happen. I can only assume that, back in 1940, this demon Shaltak somehow became linked with Judith Prendergast while Judith was still alive."

"And you'd heard of Shaltak before you came here?"

"She's mentioned in several ancient texts," he explains. "She's not a particularly notorious demon, but she's recorded as having caused trouble as far back as the time of the Sumerians and the Akkadians, which is essentially the dawn of recorded history. So I guess you could say that she's an old hand at this. Quite why and how she ended up in a church in the English countryside, I can't imagine. Maybe she just likes to travel." He sets some more books onto the table. "That was a little joke, by the way."

His hands are still shaking, and I'm starting to think that I really don't want to be here. In fact, I'm already trying to think of an excuse to leave.

"Why *you*?" I ask finally.

He glances at me.

"Why are you here, doing this all alone?" I continue. "Don't you have, like, priest friends to come and help you out? Hell, shouldn't the police know what's going on?"

"We've found that priests should work alone in these cases," he explains, "in order to avoid certain tricks that the demons like to pull. One non-priest assistant is usually fine. And you could call the police and tell them about this place, but guess what? They'd either laugh at you, or they'd refer you to the organization I work for. There's no need to -"

Suddenly there's a loud banging sound. I turn and look toward the doorway, but Liam hurries past me and looks out into the corridor.

"Well," he says after a moment, "it looks like she slammed a door. How cliched for a ghost. I think maybe she's getting angry or nervous, but she's too afraid to strike at us directly. I'll have to -"

"I don't think I can do this," I say suddenly. "I'm sorry, man, but I'm no ghost-hunter or demon-hunter. This shit's starting to feel way too real and I want out."

"Impossible."

"I'm walking out that door right now."

"You can't seriously think she'll let you do that, can you?" he asks, as he sets some empty vials on the table and then takes out a bottle of mineral water.

"Why wouldn't she?"

"Because you know about Shaltak." He pours a small amount of the water into each vial. "I made damn sure that we just talked about Shaltak here in the church, where she can overhear us. And while demons always like to hear their name, she won't want you going around telling people what's going on here in the church. She'll kill you, just like she killed Kerry. I'm sorry, Mark, but you have to stay now. I've made sure of that."

"You tricked me?" I ask, shocked by his confession.

"I made sure that I had some insurance. I bound you to this ritual, because I knew that I'd need you. I'm sorry if that upsets you, but I did what was necessary in order to ensure that the demon is cast out. If it's any consolation, the same applies to me too. I can't walk away either. Not now."

"Bullshit," I reply, pushing past him and heading out into the corridor. "I'm not falling for any more of your games." I hurry toward the closed door and reach down to grab the handle. "There's no way this -"

Stopping suddenly, I realize that there's a hand on my shoulder. I'm certain that Liam didn't follow me out of the office, at least not quickly enough to have caught me already. Just as I start trying to convince myself that it must be him, I realize I can feel the icy fingers burning through the fabric of my t-shirt, and the hairs on the back of my neck are starting to stand up. I have one hand on the door's handle, but I'm starting to feel nauseous and finally, slowly, I turn around in an attempt to prove to myself that none of this is real.

Judith Prendergast lunges at me and screams.

Pulling away, I slam against the door and then I slump to the ground, landing hard on the stone floor. I wince, but as I look up I see that there's already nobody standing over me. She was there, and then she wasn't, but I can still feel the cold patch on my shoulder.

A moment later, Liam comes out of the office and stops in the doorway. He has various books and other items in his arms.

"Okay," he says, "I think you probably understand now that I was telling the truth. Are you ready to get this job done?"

CHAPTER TWENTY-TWO
MARK

HE'S READING FROM THE book, taking care with each unintelligible word. He told me earlier that the text is in Latin, and that it has to be read in its original form, which means that I don't have a clue what he's saying. There's one word that I keep hearing, though; every couple of minutes, the demon's name is used.

"Shaltak."

Looking out across the church from the steps of the altar, I see no sign of anyone else here. The burned, ruined pews are all still in position, just about visible in the late-afternoon gloom. Rain is crashing down harder than ever outside and the light seems to be dimming, and some of the shadows here in the church are getting darker and larger. I keep watching those shadows, in case anything appears, but so far it's as if we're being left alone.

Glancing at the altar, I see the vials sitting in a row.

"Holy water," Liam explained a few hours ago, when we came through here.

"From a bottle of mineral water?"

"Any water can be blessed."

And then he held a hand against each vial, and simply announced that they were now blessed.

"It can't be that easy," I told him.

"There's nothing easy about faith," he replied. "It doesn't even matter what you have faith *in*. Faith in the power of good, in the face of evil, is just as powerful as faith in the Lord."

Now those seven vials are standing on the altar, as if they're waiting to be used. I don't really understand how this ritual is supposed to work, but I'm pretty sure that Liam's trying to summon the ghost of Judith Prendergast so that he can cast her out of the church and send her away from this world forever. So far, however, she doesn't appear to be taking the bait, and I can't help thinking that she might be too smart to fall for whatever Liam's got planned.

I guess I just have to try to have faith in him.

"How long are we going to do this?" I ask. "How long before you try something else?"

He doesn't reply. He glances at me, but he keeps on reading from the book. I suppose the book might be his only idea, and he did say earlier that this task might take a while. I feel as if he's daring the ghost to appear, as if he thinks its arrival is inevitable. To be honest, I don't see why the ghost or the demon – whatever it is – can't just hide away and wait for us to give up. Unless it can't help itself. Unless it's somehow drawn to us, and eventually it'll *have* to come.

I look over toward the shadows again.

And then I see her.

The ghost of Judith Prendergast is standing in the archway that leads through here from the corridor. She's not in the shadows at all; she's silhouetted against the corridor's stone wall, and she appears to be staring straight at us.

"Liam, she's there!" I blurt out, pulling back as I feel a ripple of panic in my chest.

He continues to read from the book.

"Liam! Look!"

He holds a hand up, as if to acknowledge that he's heard me, but he doesn't stop reading and he keeps his eyes fixed on the book.

"Fuck," I whisper under my breath, as I watch the ghost. Why's she just standing there? What does she want?

Suddenly she screams, and then she's gone.

I pull back further, all the way up the steps

until I bump into the base of the altar. I keep looking at the spot where the ghost was standing, but there's no sign of her at all. Looking around, I try to spot her anywhere else in the church, but it's as if she simply disappeared.

"Why did she do that?" I ask, turning to Liam.

Instead of replying, he simply continues to read out all that Latin stuff from the book. I flinch, and for a moment I almost reach out and snatch that stupid book straight out of his hands. I manage to hold back, however, and instead I look back across the church, trying to spot where Judith Prendergast will appear next.

"Why did she scream?" I whisper, as I try to make sense of all this shit. "I mean, she's still got a mind, right? She still thinks. Did she just do it to scare us? She was way too far away for that." I pause, as my mind races with the possibilities. "It doesn't make any fucking sense."

For the next few minutes, I continue to watch for the ghost's return. At the same time, I've got this growing feeling that I'm being watched, and finally I realize that the sensation seemed to be coming from a spot about halfway along the aisle. I take a deep breath as I try to stay calm, but I swear it feels as if – since she disappeared – the ghost of Judith Prendergast has been silently making her way along the aisle, heading straight for us.

"I know you're there," I say under my breath, as Liam continues to read out loud. Watching the empty space in the aisle, I realize I can definitely feel a gaze staring back at me, and it's as if the gaze is definitely coming this way.

I take a step back, until I'm standing right next to the altar.

"Liam, she's coming toward us," I stammer, figuring that he might not realize. "I swear to you, she's almost here now."

He reads some more of that stupid Latin bullshit.

"You'd better have something figured out," I continue, as I watch the empty space and realize that the ghost is now right at the foot of the altar, just a few feet away. My heart is pounding and I don't mind admitting that I'm terrified. "You've got more than a few books, yeah?" I ask. "Maybe it's time to sprinkle out some of that holy water."

I back away from the edge of the altar, as I sense the ghost coming up the steps.

Suddenly she appears and lunges at me, screaming again. I just have time to see her anguished, horrified face as I step back, and I feel a flash of ice-cold air as her hands reach for me.

And then she's gone again.

"Fuck," I whisper as I step back around the altar. "Liam, did you see that?"

I look around, but now I can't tell where she

is. I still feel as if I'm being watched, but I can't quite pinpoint where she's standing.

"Liam, mate," I continue, as my panic grows and grows, "I reckon we might be in a bit deep here. You've got her attention, now it's time to do whatever else you're gonna do."

I wait, before turning to him.

"Do something!" I yell, as he carries on reading. "Don't just stand there! You have to do something!"

I wait.

He keeps reading.

"Liam!"

I take a step toward him, but suddenly I feel something rushing at me from behind. I begin to turn, but in a flash I feel an icy hand grab the side of my neck and I freeze. I tell myself that this can't be what it seems like, that I have to be wrong, but then the fingers tighten their grip and when I try to turn away I find that I can't. And then, slowly, I sense something leaning over my shoulder, and I see Judith Prendergast's face staring straight into my eyes.

"Liam," I whisper, barely managing to get the words out, "please..."

"What are you doing in my church?" the ghost asks. "Who invited you here?"

I try to answer, but I can't get any words out. And then, slowly, I realize that Liam has finally stopped speaking.

"This is my church and you have no right to be here," the ghost continues. "You must leave at once, you are not -"

Suddenly she screams again, lunging at me before vanishing.

Falling forward, I slump down against the stone floor, only for Liam to grab me by the shoulders and haul me up.

"What happened?" he asks. "Did you see her?"

"She was talking to me," I stammer, turning and looking back at the spot where Judith Prendergast was standing. "She screamed at me."

"You cried out," he replies.

I turn to him.

"You were asking why I'm in your church," he continues cautiously, "and then you shouted. Like a scream, maybe. Mark, is this like what happened to your friend Kerry?"

"I'm getting out of here," I say, turning to run, only for him to grab my hand and hold me back.

"We're halfway there!" he hisses.

"I don't care!" I try to pull free, but he grabs my arm and shoves me hard against the altar. "I don't want to be here!"

"She won't let you leave," he replies, before hurrying back past the altar and grabbing the bottles of holy water. "I can't do anything when she's speaking through you," he continues. "It has to be sooner than that. Mark, is she here now? Can you sense her?"

Looking around, all I feel is pure, cold panic.

"Tell me!" Liam shouts. "This is not the moment to flake out on me, Mark! Where is she?"

"I don't think she's here," I reply, looking all around but still not sensing anything. "Man, I think she's gone. I think we should leave before she comes back."

"Focus!" he snaps. "She didn't just walk away. She's here somewhere."

"She had me," I point out, turning to him. "Why did she scream and let me go?"

"I don't know," he replies, "but it's not important right now. All that matters is working out where she is right now, and then I can do the rest. Stay calm, Mark, and find her. I know how these things work, she won't have gone far."

I look around again, but there's still no sign of her. Then, as I turn back to Liam and open my mouth to tell him that this is all hopeless, I realize that I *can* sense her. She's staring straight at me, and she's doing it from the space right behind Liam's left shoulder.

"Well?" he asks. "Anything?"

"She's here," I stammer.

"Where? I need to know exactly."

I swallow hard.

"Where is she?" he shouts.

"Right behind you," I tell him. "She's right behind you. Your left shoulder."

He pauses, and I can see the fear in his eyes. Then, slowly, he begins to open the lid of one of the vials. His hands are shaking and I can tell that he's scared, but after a moment he drops the lid and holds the vial up.

"Be ready," he says, his voice shaking with fear.

"What -"

Suddenly he tosses the holy water over his shoulder and runs forward. Immediately, the face of Judith Prendergast appears behind him and screams, as if she's in pain as the holy water falls against her.

By the time Liam reaches me and turns to look, the face is already gone again.

"I don't think she liked that," I tell him.

"She's part-demon," he replies, as we both watch the space where the face appeared. "Holy water burns. Do you still sense her there?"

"No," I reply, before realizing that maybe I *can* feel that we're being watched.

I turn slowly, looking out into the gloom, and then I point at one particular spot.

"There!" I shout.

Liam throws some more holy water in that

direction. Judith's face appears again, screaming and wracked with pain, lunging toward us for a moment before vanishing again.

"She's trapped," Liam explains. "She knows she has to stop us now, but the holy water is wearing her down. One more time should be enough, but you have to remain vigilant. If she gets close to use again, we might not be able to fight her off. Mark, where is she now?"

"I don't know," I reply, still frantically looking around.

"You do!" he snaps. "You just have to stay focused!"

"She's not here!"

"Yes, she is!"

"If she was here, I'd be able to -"

Suddenly I spin around, and in an instant I can tell that I'm being watched from the shadows beyond the altar.

"There!" I shout, and I point at the exact spot.

Liam rushes forward and throws another vial holy water past the altar. Immediately, Judith Prendergast appears and screams, rushing forward only to fall and disappear down behind the altar.

I take a step back.

"Why does she keep vanishing like that?" I ask. "How are we going to get her if..."

My voice trails off as I realize I can hear a

faint sobbing sound coming from the other side of the altar. I look over at Liam, but he's staring at the altar as if he doesn't quite understand what's happening. I wait, hoping that he'll spring into action and explain everything, and finally he takes a cautious step around the altar's far side.

Realizing that I have to know what's happening, I make my way around the altar's other side, until we both stop and look down at the shocking sight of Judith Prendergast kneel on the stone floor, weeping with her face in her hands.

I look at Liam, hoping for a cue, but he's simply staring down at the sobbing ghost.

"What's wrong with her?" I ask, as I feel a crippling fear in my chest. "What happened?"

As I say those words, Judith Prendergast slowly lifts her face and looks first at Liam and then at me. She looks different now, less evil and more like a regular person. In fact, the more she cries, the more she looks desperately sad.

"No," she whimpers, and now her whole body is shaking, "please, you don't understand..."

"Don't let her get close to you," Liam tells me, as he holds up the last vial of holy water.

"Help me," she sobs, as she starts crawling toward me and reaches out a hand. "I'm begging you..."

"Don't let her touch you!" Liam shouts, before stepping up behind the ghost.

"Please," she cries, "you have to help me! I'm so sorry for what I did, but you have to understand, I tried to hold her back! I tried to stop her! I was always -"

Suddenly she rushes at me and screams, but Liam throws the last of the holy water at her and she cries out. I step back against the wall, and in the very last moment the ghost of Judith Prendergast vanishes into thin air.

I wait, terrified, and then finally Liam drops the vial.

"She's gone," he says, and now he sounds exhausted. "The holy water was enough. I wasn't sure it would be, but I suspect her sense of shame was enough to make her finally leave. Either that, or she couldn't stand the water as it fell upon her. Whatever. The most important thing is that she's gone."

"And she can't come back?" I ask, turning to him.

He pauses, before shaking his head.

"She's gone forever," he says with a sigh, still staring at the spot where we last saw the ghost. "She's gone to the same place as your friend Kerry. Wherever that might be."

CHAPTER TWENTY-THREE
MARK

"SO WHAT HAPPENS NOW?" I ask as I drop the last of the empty vials into Liam's bag. "To the church, I mean."

All I hear is the sound of rain lashing against the stained-glass windows. After a moment, realizing that Liam hasn't replied, I turn to see that he's standing close to the altar and looking out across the burned pews.

"Can it just open again?" I continue. "Can the people of Briarwych start to use it?"

"Huh?" He turns to me, and it's clear that he wasn't paying attention. "The church? Oh, yes, I suppose so. There'll be superstitions aplenty, I'm sure, and it'll take a while for those to blow over. I imagine some of the locals will never be persuaded to give the place a try, but that's just how people are."

"I bet Caroline and Brian will refuse," I reply. "They seem totally -"

Before I can finish, I hear a bumping sound coming from out in the corridor. I turn and look toward the arched doorway, but now the church has fallen silent again.

"Did you hear that?" I ask.

"Hear what?"

"There was a sound again," I tell him. "I'm not lying, I swear."

"I'm sure this time it was just something innocuous," he replies. "I know it's something of a cliche, Mark, but this really is a very old building. Parts of it date back as far as the twelfth century. Maybe what you heard was just the foundations settling a little."

"Yeah, but..."

I watch the archway for a moment longer, before reminding myself that I really need to listen to Liam. After all, he's been right about everything so far.

"So what happened to the demon?" I ask, turning to him. "Did it just vanish after you got rid of Judith Prendergast's ghost?"

"What do you mean?"

"You said she'd become one with the demon, right?"

"Right."

"And you got rid of Judith, but did the demon go with her? 'Cause just now, when we saw her, she didn't seem very demonic."

"You can't always judge such things from appearances alone, Mark."

"She didn't sound very demonic, either."

"To be honest, this is a situation I've never encountered before," he says. "Nor have I heard of anything quite like this. But if Judith and Shaltak were entwined, it stands to reason that getting rid of one would get rid of the other. The demon was anchored here by Judith, and now the anchor is gone. I see no reason why the demon would still be here. Don't you agree?"

"I guess so," I reply, but I'm still a little worried about something. "Why was she sobbing?"

"Judith?" He closes the zipper on his bag. "Fear, perhaps," he continues. "Maybe she realized that once she was forced out of the church, she'd be gone forever. After all, as you pointed out, she consistently referred to this as *her* church. I imagine it was quite a wrench for her to realize that she wouldn't be able to haunt the place forever."

"Is that really all she wanted?"

"You think there was something else?"

"It just doesn't seem like much motivation, that's all."

"There was an element of revenge, as well,"

he continues. "Maybe she was expecting to one day -"

Suddenly there's another bumping sound, and I turn just in time to see that one of the farthest pews seems to have shifted slightly. I might not know much, but I'm pretty sure that wasn't the sound of any foundations settling.

"What was that?" I ask, turning back to Liam.

He watches the pews for a few seconds, before glancing at me and then grabbing his jacket from the floor.

"I'm sure it was nothing," he says, forcing a smile. "You won't get over this experience quickly, Mark. I remember the first time I encountered such things. I was nervous and jumpy for months, and my view of the world had been changed forever. You now know that demons and ghosts are real, which means that your understanding of the world has changed rather radically. Not many people have the knowledge that you've acquired. I can help you, if you like. You don't have to face this challenge alone."

"We should tell people."

"Tell them?"

"About all of it! Everyone has a right to know that this kind of shit is real!"

"I'm not sure that would be very wise," he says cautiously. "Can you imagine the panic?

242

Society isn't ready for that information."

"Is that why you're offering to help me, then?" I ask. "Is it just part of your attempt to cover it all up?"

"I'm offering to help because I think you *need* help. You've been through a lot, Mark, and my understanding is that you're alone in the world. I work for an organization that has financial wherewithal to assist you."

"I don't want anything to do with any of this," I tell him, "or with any organization. I just -"

Suddenly there's another bang, and I turn to see that the two long pews on the back row have both been pushed aside by some unseen force.

"You saw that," I stammer, as I realize that there's definitely something still here in the church. "You can't tell me you didn't!"

"Wait a moment," he says, and I can hear him stepping up behind me.

"No, don't lie, you saw it!" I shout, and then I turn to him. "Liam, you -"

Before I can finish, something sharp digs into my belly. Letting out a gasp, I step back and look down, and to my horror I see that Liam is holding a small, bloodied knife in his right hand. And as I stare at the blood that's already dripping from the blade's edge, I feel a growing pain in my gut. Looking at the front of my shirt, I see blood soaking through the fabric around a large, gashed rip.

"What..."

"I'm sorry, Mark," Liam says, before grabbing my shoulder and pulling me closer.

I try to cry out, but he stabs me again, this time pushing the blade in all the way and then twisting it hard.

"You're a good kid," he continues, "and it's a shame you got caught up in all of this, but I can't help that. Just know that I'm really, *really* sorry for everything."

With that, he pulls the knife out, and then he shoves me hard. I try to step back, but instead I fall and clatter down the stone steps until I land in a heap on the floor at the head of the aisle. I try to get up, but the pain in my belly is intense and then I freeze as I see two more of the pews getting ripped up from the ground and sent clattering through the air until they smash against the walls. Then two more pews are tossed aside, then two more, with each row getting blasted away as if something is coming closer and closer toward us.

"She's coming," Liam says behind me. "I finally did it. I finally freed Shaltak from this wretched place."

CHAPTER TWENTY-FOUR
MARK

THE NEAREST SET OF pews flies up into the air. I look up, horrified, as they slam into the church's high vaulted ceiling and are then sent thudding into opposite walls. Turning, I watch as one of the pews shatters against the stone and then falls to the floor, and then I feel something brush against my shoulder.

Shivering with fear, I turn and look up. I don't see anything, but I swear I can sense a presence moving up the steps and going to join Liam at the altar.

"Let's have some light," Liam says as he lights a couple of large candles, brightening the gloom as rain continues to fall outside. "It's getting cold in here as well, don't you think?"

Turning, I try to drag myself along the aisle, but I immediately stop as I feel a tightening, burning pain in my gut. I wince and try to find the strength to keep going, and then I reach out and try to pull myself a little way from the altar. The pain immediately returns, however, and I let out a faint whimper as I slump back down. I can feel hot blood soaking the front of my shirt, and I'm already starting to get weak.

"I freed you!" Liam calls out behind me. "You called for help, and I answered. You killed the girl and then you let the boy go, so that he could tell others. You knew someone like me would respond, that I'd come here. I know you'd become entwined with the ghost of Judith Prendergast, that she was desperately holding you back and preventing you from escaping. I'm surprised that a foolish woman was able to do that, but I suppose she was frantic. She's gone now, though. I've banished her, so you're free. Of all the men in this world, I'm the only one who came to serve you. I'm your truest follower."

After taking a series of slow, steady breaths, I get ready to drag myself again. This time I know it's going to hurt, but I figure I can force my way through the pain, so I reach out and steady myself on my elbows and then I drag myself along the aisle.

The pain is so intense, I scream for several seconds, and finally I slump back down just half a meter from where I started. Whimpering as the pain ripples through my belly, I can feel tears in my eyes.

"I bow down before you with but one request," Liam continues. "Return my wife to me. She was a good woman, and she was cut down in the cruelest manner possible. Until that moment, I believed that good would always overcome evil. I still believe there is good out there somewhere, but it has abandoned us. And if we have been abandoned, then we must serve whatever masters remain. Please, Shaltak, I beg you, grant me this meager reward in recognition of all that I have done for you. It's all I ask."

I can do this.

I can drag myself to the corridor and then out of the church, and I can call for help. I don't know whose job it is to come and deal with demons. Liam didn't exactly do too well, but I guess he went a little rogue. Whoever sent Liam can send someone else, and then this Shaltak asshole will be sent away. And then, I guess, the whole world's going to have to reckon with the fact that demons are real.

After taking a moment to gather some strength, I reach out to steady myself. At the last moment, however, I glance over my shoulder, and to my horror I see that Liam isn't alone at the altar. Caught in the flickering candlelight, he's on his knees as a dark figure towers over him. The candlelight briefly grows a little, revealing the twisted, hate-filled face of Judith Prendergast. The demon must have kept her form, even now that the ghost herself is gone, and I watch as she stares down at Liam with an expression of disgust.

"No-one else came to help you," Liam tells her. "I'm the only one. The rest of them saw you as something to be feared, something to be contained here in the church, but I recognized your power. I saw that you -"

Before he can finish, Shaltak screams. The candles are blown out, and I watch as Liam is thrown through the air. He cries out as he rushes past me, and I turn just in time to see him slam into the wall next to the archway. As his body crumples down to the floor, I can already see that he's broken.

Filled with fear, I start dragging myself along the aisle, trying desperately to get to the archway and to then reach the door. Every inch of movement is agony, but I manage to shuffle along on my elbows until finally I reach Liam's body. He's shivering on the floor, and I hear the creaking of broken bones as he turns to me and tries to get up.

"I just wanted to get her back," he sobs. "I have to make Shaltak see that I'm worthy."

He reaches out to grab me, but I pull my arm away.

"I understand why you hate me," he continues, "but I did what I had to do. You've never been in love, Mark. You don't know what it's like."

"You're a liar!" I spit back at him.

"I prayed so long and so hard for my wife," he says, as a dribble of blood runs from the corner of his mouth, "and she still died. She still suffered for so long as the cancer ate her away. Then, when she was gone, I prayed for some sign that she was waiting for me, that I'd see her again if I ended my life. After a while, Mark, praying into silence feels hopeless. So I decided to worship something that might actually talk back to me. To something that might actually acknowledge what I've been through. To something that might actually help."

"Everything you said was bullshit!" I shout. "You used me!"

"I told you what I *used* to believe," he replies, before looking past me.

Turning, I see that the dark figure of Judith Prendergast has come down from the altar and is now slowly stalking toward us. Whereas the ghost was, at times, quite frail-looking, the demon form stands tall and menacing, and I can feel the floor shaking slightly beneath me with each step that the creature takes this way.

"What does it want?" I ask.

"To cause trouble," Liam replies. "To hurt people. To watch people suffer."

"And you chose to release it?"

"I've spent years trying to do the right

thing," he explains, "and all that time, I was aware of the Briarwych case. I knew there was something trapped here in the church, something that could help me. At first I dismissed the idea, but gradually I began to think more and more about coming here to Briarwych and releasing Shaltak. Then, when I heard about your friend's death, I realized that maybe the demon knew that I was out there, or at least that *someone* was out there. She was sending a message, hoping that someone would come and release her. I answered that call. I gave her what she wanted. I'm sorry I lied to you earlier. I already suspected that Shaltak would be here."

"You abandoned everything you used to believe in!"

"I still believe in part of it," Liam continues. "I believe that there's good out there somewhere. But wherever it is, it's too far away for any of us to feel it. So why not turn to the bad instead? Why not barter and negotiate with these creatures, to get what we want? That's the problem with pure faith. After a while, it just wears you down."

"Or maybe you never really felt it in the first place," I reply, watching as the demon gets closer and closer, then turning to Liam again. "Maybe you were full of hot air."

"Maybe I'm just a man who wants his wife back," he says, "and who'll do anything to get her."

He looks along the aisle.

Following his gaze, I turn and see that Shaltak is getting closer and closer.

"She has to bring her back for me," Liam whimpers, his voice filled with sobs now. "That's what all of this is for. She has to bring her back!"

Turning, I start dragging myself through the arched doorway and out into the corridor, and then toward the main door. I can hear rain still crashing down outside, and I know that I have to get out of this church before that creature gets to me. Realizing that crawling isn't going to be fast enough, I reach up and put a hand against the cold stone wall, and then I take a moment to steady myself. For a few seconds I feel weak again, as if I can't keep going. As if I can only stay down here on the ground and wait to die.

"I bow down before you!" Liam shouts behind me. "You're free now! You've been trapped in this church for more than seventy years, but now you can leave! You can do whatever you want in the world, and in return I ask only that you grant me the one thing that I need. Please, bring her back. I know she didn't just vanish into nothingness after she died. Her soul has to be somewhere. Bring her back, I -"

Suddenly he lets out a gurgled, agonized cry.

I force myself up, tottering on my unsteady legs, and then I limp toward the door.

Behind me, Liam is still crying out. I don't know what Shaltak is doing to him, but somehow I get the feeling that there aren't going to be any rewards tonight. Reaching the door, I wince as I feel the pain bursting up from my gut, but then I force myself to keep going. I start pulling the door open, and almost immediately I feel cold wind and rain blasting against my face. I take a step forward, determined to get out there and call for help, but at the very last moment I stop, and then I make a terrible mistake.

I turn and look back, to see what's happening to Liam.

Shaltak is gripping the sides of Liam's face and is slowly ripping his head free from his body. Liam's struggling and trying to fight back, but already part of his neck has been torn open and I can see blood spraying out across the darkness. And then, as I continue to watch, I see his head being lifted higher, until strings of flesh are just about visible clinging either side of the exposed upper section of his spine. Still gasping, still shaking, Liam lets out a pained gurgle as his head is lifted even further from his neck, and finally the last pieces of connecting flesh and bone are broken.

In the darkness, I can just about see that Liam's eyes are still blinking.

Suddenly Shaltak starts crushing the head, squeezing it hard until I hear the skull crack.

Turning, I limp out into the rain, which is so strong that it almost knocks me straight back down. I stop and look out toward the lights of the village, but I don't see anyone nearby.

"Help!" I call out, but I already know that nobody will be able to hear me over the sound of the rain.

Hoping against hope that Shaltak isn't ready to follow me just yet, I hurry out across the cemetery, limping as fast as I can through the rain.

CHAPTER TWENTY-FIVE
MARK

"HELP!" I SHOUT, CLUTCHING my bloodied belly as I limp along the street. "Somebody help me!"

It's dark now, and rain is crashing down. Reaching the first cottage in a row, I stumble through the garden gate and start banging my fists on the door.

"Help me!" I yell. "Call for help! You have to get someone here!"

I look over my shoulder, but there's no sign of anything or anyone following me. Turning back to the door, I bang again, and then I look at the window and see that there's a light in the front room.

I wait, and then I limp back out of the

garden and along to the next cottage. I need to find someone who's actually home.

"Help!" I shout, slamming into the next door and then banging with both fists. "You have to call for help!"

Again I wait. For a moment, I think I hear movement on the other side of the door, but then there's nothing other than silence. With rain still falling all around, I'm drenched and shivering now, and finally I knock again on the door.

"Please!" I sob. "Somebody open the door!"

Realizing that maybe there's nobody home here either, I limp back out onto the road. I take a moment to look back toward the church. For a few seconds I see nothing but the dark lane winding up the hill, but then I spot something moving in the darkness. Panicking, I turn and start hurrying along the lane, and finally I spot the Neills' cottage up ahead. I manage to speed up, and somehow I'm able to reach their front door.

"Help!" I shout as I start pounding on the door. "It's me! You have to open the door!"

Spotting movement at the window, I turn just in time to see Brian Neill staring at me from the other side of the rain-spattered window. And then, suddenly, Caroline Neil steps into view behind him and pulls the curtain shut.

"Are you kidding?" I stammer, before starting to hammer the door again. "I'm hurt! It's out of the church! I need help, you have to let me in!"

I bang on the door for what feels like an eternity, until finally stepping back as I realize that they're not going to let me inside. Stepping back onto the road, I look at the row of cottages and see that most of them have lights on in their windows. Despite the rain, these people must be able to hear me, they must know what's going on out here. And then, one by one, the windows start to fall dark, as if the people inside simply want to pretend that there's nobody home.

"Come on," I whisper, horrified to realize that even now they're not going to acknowledge what's happening. "What's wrong with you all?"

Looking back along the road, I tell myself that there's nothing there, that nothing's coming for me through the darkness. After a few seconds, however, I spot something moving along the lane, and somehow deep down I instantly know that it's the creature from the church.

I turn to run, but at that moment I spot Brian's bike resting against the garden wall. I rush over and grab the bike, swinging it over the wall, and then – despite the pain in my belly – I climb on and start pedaling. Bursts of agony dart up across belly and into my chest every time I move my right leg, but I know that the creature will catch me if I stop. So I force myself to ride, moving slowly but surely along the dark street, and finally I manage to pick up the pace a little. By the time I've reached the bottom of the lane, I know what I have to do.

Nobody in Briarwych is going to help me. They're all too fucking scared, and too used to hiding away in their cute little cottages. Which means I have to go and find help somewhere else.

I take the next left and start cycling out of the village. I know the way to Crenford, although I'm not sure I can make it that far. I'm sure there must be other villages along the way, however, and maybe a few scattered houses in the countryside. Once I'm out of Briarwych, I can find someone who's not a goddamn coward, and I can get help. I glance over my shoulder, but there's no sign of anything following me so I look ahead and start pedaling as hard as I can, trying to push through the pain.

After a few minutes I reach the crossroads just outside the village. There's a sign, but in the dark I can't make out anything that it says. I look around, and the only lights are from Briarwych behind me. And then, suddenly, I realize I can hear something just a short way off in the distance. Something's coming this way, moving quickly through the darkness. I can't see it, but I can feel it watching me, the same way I felt it watching me in the church.

I turn and start riding again, speeding as fast as I can manage along the pitch-black road, struggling to even make out where the road ends and the grass verge begins. For the next few minutes I keep expecting to hit a patch of grass and go flying, but somehow I'm just about able to spot each turn as it arrives. I don't dare turn and look back, and I have to focus on trying to burn through the pain. I don't know how I'm managing to ride with a stab wound in my guts, but I keep telling myself that any other choice means instant death.

And then a little while later, just as I feel as if I can't go on, I spot a light ahead.

It's just a small pinprick, burning in the darkness, but at least it's something. Realizing that I've found a house, I start pedaling faster, and after a couple of minutes I see a couple more lights beyond a distant treeline. Whatever fucked-up shit is going on in Briarwych, it can't have reached this far outside the village, so I keep going until I reach a turn-off that heads toward the lights and then I start cycling that way. All I have to do is get help, and make sure someone calls the police and the authorities, and then everything will be okay.

Reaching a fence, I find that there's an old wooden barrier in the way. I dismount and duck under the barrier, pulling the bike through too, and then I climb back on and reach my foot down to start pedaling again. At the last second, however, I stop as I look ahead, and I realize where I am.

I'm at the old airbase, except it no longer

looks abandoned. There are lights along the runway, and more lights in one of the buildings. I don't know why or how, but suddenly there are people here.

"Hey!" I yell, before realizing that in the wind and rain they're never going to hear me.

I start cycling furiously toward the building. As I reach the runway, I see that there are regular lights on either side, marking the way. The bike's tires almost slip in the rain, but I manage to keep going until finally I get to the building. After climbing off the bike, I pull open a door on the side of the building and then I run inside. The corridor is well lit and I can hear voices in one of the rooms ahead. A man is barking out orders, and other men are replying to him. I don't know what they're on about, but finally I reach the doorway and hurry into the room.

"Help!" I shout. "There's a -"

In that instant, the voices stop and the light goes, and I'm left standing in the darkness.

As rain pounds against the roof, I look around and see that the place is exactly how it was when I first came here a few weeks ago. It's clear that that building was abandoned long ago, and there's no way a bunch of people can have just vanished in the blink of an eye.

Spotting an old-fashioned phone on a desk, I hurry over and pick up the receiver, but of course there's no signal. I try a couple more times, just in case by some miracle the phone might connect, but then I set it down as I realize that there's nothing here that can help me. I have to get back on the bike and keep going.

Hurrying back outside, I pick the bike up and try to climb on, only for a sudden pain to twist in my gut. I almost fall, but I just about manage to stay upright. I can't quite clamber onto the bike's seat, however, so for a few paces I simply push the bike and limp along until I'm at the edge of the runway. The lights are still burning on either side, but as I try to climb back onto the bike I feel another burst of pain and I once again have to stop for a moment.

Then, looking ahead, I see her.

Judith Prendergast is standing just a few feet away, staring at me.

Or rather, the demon is there, still twisted into her form.

I try again to climb onto the bike. This time the pain is even stronger, and I slip on the wet ground. Falling, I slam down hard and the bike lands on top of me. I let out a gasp of pain, but I immediately start getting up and try once more to get onto the bike.

I fall again, landing even harder, and then I get up. I raise my right leg to mount the bike, but the pain is too much and I stumble forward before falling. The bike clatters to the ground behind me.

Reaching down, I feel the soaking wet, freezing cold front of my shirt. As I move my hands down, however, my fingertips brush against a warmer patch where blood has caked the fabric against my wound.

My knees are trembling as I get back to my feet. And then, before I even have a chance to turn and grab the bike, my legs give way beneath me and I fall back down, landing hard on my knees and then slumping forward onto my elbows.

Shivering in the rain, I realize this time that I'm not going to be able to get back up. I try, but something's locked my body in place, as if the pain has finally become too much. After a few deep breaths, I manage to sit up slightly, but I don't think I'm ever going to be able to get back onto my feet again.

Staring up, I look into the face of this demon creature that followed me out here from the church.

"What do you want?" I yell, as rain continues to crash down all around us. "If you want to kill me, just get it over with, okay?"

I wait, but the demon simply stares at me. There's a dark mark on one side of Judith's face, and I think that's a wound caused by the holy water that hit her earlier.

And then she starts to laugh.

"I give up," I continue. "You've won, so just

get it over with. Can't you just do to me, what you did to Kerry? That didn't seem so painful."

She laughs for a moment longer, before stepping toward me and reaching out. I feel an icy hand against the side of my face, and then she slowly tilts my head up as she leans down toward me.

"Do it!" I sneer, as I wait for the inevitable. "Just fucking do it, okay?"

Grinning from ear to ear, she tilts her head slightly as she runs a fingertip down the side of my face and onto my throat.

"Do it!" I shout, but it's clear that she's savoring the moment. "You fucking ugly, piece of shit demon trash, get it over with and kill me! Or are you too scared? Are you too much of a fucking pussy?"

Still, she doesn't do it. She's enjoying this far too much, but I'm not going to give her the satisfaction of seeing my fear, so finally I close my eyes and wait. I'm sure that, now she's out of the church, this monster has way more important things to be doing, so now she'll have to just get the job done. As the seconds pass, I keep my eyes squeezed tight shut and wait for the end.

And then I realize I can hear a plane approaching.

I hesitate, convinced that I must be wrong, but I swear I can hear an engine getting louder and louder over the sound of the rain. Finally I open my eyes, and I see that Shaltak has turned her head slightly, as if she's heard the same thing. A moment later I spot a growing patch of light in the sky, as if something's roaring toward us from the far end of the runway, from somewhere behind Shaltak. It's almost as if...

Suddenly a small plane races right above us, missing us by just a few feet. Shaltak lets go of me and I fall down, turning as I land. I see the plane bouncing as it hits the runway, and then it slows fast and turns slightly before coming to a halt. There are lights in the building again, and I spot shadowy figures racing out to meet the plane.

"What the hell?" I whisper.

"Get him out of there!" I hear a man shouting in the distance. "Hurry up, we need to get him into the sickbay!"

"We took some heavy fire over Calais!" another man yells. "Where's Bolton?"

"He's coming!"

I watch the shadows for a moment. Despite the rain, I can just about make our figures silhouetted against the building's lights, and it looks like they're carrying a man down from the plane. Then I spot another figure hurrying out from the building, and he stops to watch as the injured man is carried past.

"Get on with it, man!" a new voices yells.

"That's an order!"

Turning, I look up at Shaltak and see that she's watching the men with a puzzled expression. She seems totally focused on them, almost as if she's forgotten that I'm down here as the rain comes crashing down. I swear, it's raining so hard, I think I could almost drown right now.

"I don't care about excuses!" the man shouts in the distance. "Find a way and get it done!"

I open my mouth to yell at Shaltak, but at the last moment I remember something Liam told me earlier today. For a few seconds the idea seems ridiculous, as if it could never work, but then I tell myself that I have to at least try.

"I bless the rain!" I shout.

Shaltak turns and looks back down at me.

"I bless all this rain!" I continue. "I bless it and turn it into holy water, in the name of... God, or something! I'm not a priest, but I can still bless it! Liam told me it's about believing, and right now I believe in good beating evil so I bless all this rain and it's gonna burn you back to Hell, motherfucker!"

Shaltak tilts her head slightly, eyeing me with a hint of confusion.

"I believe in good things," I stammer, as I start to feel weaker and weaker. "I believe that good beats evil. That's what I believe in. I believe in all that kind of stuff, I swear I do, so I bless the rain."

With the last of my strength, I reach my right hand up and open my fist to feel the rain fully. "I'm turning it into holy water with my faith!" I shout. "So suck on that, bitch!"

I wait.

Shaltak stares at me, as the voices continue to shout in the distance. And then, slowly, the smile returns to Shaltak's face and she starts laughing.

"I'm blessing the rain!" I yell, figuring that it just must take a little time. "I swear!"

Still laughing, she reaches down and grabs the side of my face again, and then she lifts me up until I can see straight into her dark eyes. With her other hand, she runs a finger against my throat, and now I can tell that she's preparing to finish me off.

"I'm blessing the rain!" I gasp, barely able to get the words out.

The voices of the ghosts are still shouting nearby.

"For Kerry," I add. "I'm blessing the rain for Kerry, because despite everything that's happened I still believe she's out there somewhere. I don't even *believe* it. I *know* it."

I wait, in case that might have done the trick, but as Shaltak continues to grin at me I realize that this whole idea was a bust anyway.

"Do what you want," I say finally. "I still know it's true."

Snarling, Shaltak starts digging her

fingertips into my throat. And then, suddenly, she stops and the smile fades from her lips, and I see fear in her eyes. At the same time, her grip on my face is starting to weaken, and I can feel her almost dropping me back down to the ground. She seems to be struggling slightly, trying but failing to dig deeper into my throat and finish me off. As the rain continues to pour down all around us, I can see that something's wrong.

And then she screams.

Letting go of me, Shaltak turns as if to run away, but then she slumps down against the tarmac. She tries to get back up, but her hunched back trembles slightly. She cries out again, but the rain seems to be burning her all over and when she raises her face I see that the rain is actually eating her away, almost as if it's some kind of acid. She tilts her head and cries out, but her jaw is already gone and her eyes seem to be melting away. As she howls with pain and tries once again to get back up, the rain pushes her back down until she collapses against the runway, and then I watch in horror as the rest of her body is washed away in the pouring rain.

I wait, convinced that somehow she's going to come back, but after a couple of minutes I realize that she's really, truly gone.

Turning, I open my mouth to call out to the airmen, but then I see that they're gone. All the lights are off, even the ones that were lining either side of the runway. I'm all alone out here.

I try to get up, but the pain in my belly is too strong and I can't even get my legs to work. I try again, but this time I slump down onto my back and I realize I'm not going to make it. Staring up into the rain, I take a series of slow, deep breaths as I wait for the end. Each breath is more painful than the last. The last thing I think, before I start to slip away, is that I was right all along. I really *would* have made a good soldier. I mean, I basically followed that guy's orders and kept fighting, even though he was a ghost. I would have made a hell of an airman.

And then the lights return.

I can't help but smile. My eyes are barely open now, but I can see the lights slowly getting brighter and I can feel a faint rumble in the tarmac beneath my body, and I guess maybe if I turned my head I'd be able to see that those ghosts are back now. In some strange way, that makes me feel good. In another life I'd have been a damn good airman, and maybe the ghosts are here because somehow they recognize me as one of their own. Maybe this is where I always belonged.

I close my eyes.

"Are you okay?" a woman yells suddenly, leaning over me.

I open my eyes wide, and then a man leans

over me as well.

"Is your name Mark?" the man asks, and now I can feel them checking my wrist for a pulse. "It's okay, Mark, we're going to get you to the hospital."

"He has an abdominal stab wound," the woman says. "We need to get him into the ambulance."

I manage to turn my head slightly, just enough to see that this time the flashing lights are coming from the back of an ambulance that's somehow driven out here.

"I'll get the stretcher," the woman mutters as she disappears from view.

"I told them it was worth checking this out," the man says as he starts lifting the front of my shirt, pulling the fabric away from the wound. "They said it was all a practical joke, but I felt it in my bones, I knew something else was going on. You're a very lucky boy. I don't know who put all those post-it notes in the office, telling us to come out here and save someone named Mark, but you're damn lucky that I was on a shift tonight. Everyone else said to ignore those notes, but I told them I had a hunch. Let's see who's laughing when we get back to Crenford, huh?"

For the next few minutes, the man and woman continue to work on me. I stare up at the sky, as rain continues to fall, and then finally I'm lifted up onto a trolley. There's pain, of course, but I think I've been given some kind of sedative and I can feel myself slipping away. As I'm wheeled toward the ambulance, however, I can't help wondering who could have left a load of post-it notes at the hospital, and who would have even know that I was out here. I know the idea's crazy, but is it possible that somehow Kerry wrote those notes to save me? Is it possible that she came back?

I choose to believe that she did.

EPILOGUE
MARK

Five years later

THE BELL RINGS OUT loud and clear, as people continue to emerge from the church and make their way across the neatly-mown cemetery.

I can't believe how much Briarwych has changed since the last time I was here. I did a little research online and found that almost all the cottages have changed hands over the past few years, and I certainly don't recognize any of the people who are coming out of the church. A few minutes ago I knocked on the door of the Neills' old cottage, and a man told me that they'd moved away. I guess the former inhabitants of Briarwych couldn't cope with the idea that the church might be safe again, but the new arrivals certainly seem happy.

"Can I help you with anything?"

Turning, I see that the local priest has come over to join me.

"Oh, I'm fine, thanks," I reply, taking a step back. I hadn't really intended to intrude. "I was just watching."

"Father Nathan Prior," he says, reaching a hand out to me. "You're a military man, I see."

"Oh, this?" I look down at my uniform for a moment, and then I shake the priest's hand. "Yeah. I mean, sort of. I do fire prevention work at airbases around the world. It's pretty cool. Lots of travel, you know?"

"And what brings you to Briarwych?" he asks.

"Well, I..."

For a moment, I consider telling him. I'm sure even the newcomers know the story of how a kid was found close to death out at the old airbase, and about how the body of Father Liam Dermott was found inside the church. Then again, I know Father Dermott's employers came to the village and took control of the investigation, and that the police were only too happy to not be involved. I remember a priest coming to the hospital and being very nice to me, and telling me that he'd help me out in exchange for my silence. He assured me that everything was now fine in Briarwych, and standing here now I guess he was right.

"I shall leave you to your thoughts," Father Prior tells me as he turns to go back over to the church. "I hope you enjoy your time in our humble village."

"Is it really okay in there now?" I blurt out suddenly.

He turns to me again.

I look at the church's wooden door, and I feel a shiver in my chest as I remember how cold it was inside, and how creeped-out I always felt.

"I mean, is it really okay?" I continue, still watching the door. "Is it all over?"

"Well, young man," the priest says cautiously, "why don't you come inside and see for yourself?"

***

"It's really cool," I say a few minutes later, as I walk along the corridor and stop to look at the far wall. "There's nothing here."

It's true. The place feels completely different, as if some invisible darkness has been lifted. I remember how I felt myself being watched when I was here before, but that's completely gone now. Instead, Briarwych Church seems completely normal, and it's clear that the place has really come to life. There are vases of flowers on a table, along with leaflets and even an information board that gives details of various events here.

Stepping over to the arched doorway, I see rows of brand new pews, and then I notice that the altar appears to have been given something of a refurbishment as well. Beautiful red curtains are hanging from one of the walls, and the feel of the church just feels completely fresh. It's hard to believe that anything bad ever happened here.

Looking down at the spot where Shaltak once scratched her name into the stonework, I see that somebody has rubbed the marks away.

"I suppose you've heard the stories about this place," the priest says.

I turn to him.

"People turn up occasionally, hoping to poke around the place," he continues. "I tell them the same thing that I'm going to tell you. Whatever happened her at Briarwych is over now. It's in the past, and I'm very much in favor of looking ahead to a bright and prosperous future. I've been here for a few years now, I was responsible for the church's re-opening. And I can assure you, as God is my witness, that the evil has passed from this place. Ask anyone in the village. People are no longer afraid."

"I can see that," I tell him. "I'm sorry, I didn't come to stir anything up."

"You're Mr. Duffley, aren't you?"

"How did you know?"

"I thought I recognized you outside. I trust that you're fully recovered from your injuries?"

"Completely."

"That's good to hear. I often wondered if you'd ever come back to see the place."

"I never planned to," I reply. "I don't even know why I came. I was just in the area, and I figured I should lay some ghosts to rest."

"I don't believe there *are* any ghosts here anymore."

"No, there aren't." I look around the room again, and it's still hard to believe how much the church has changed. "I should go," I add finally, turning to the priest. "I have a train to catch."

"Let me walk you out."

As we head to the door, I feel strangely calm. For the past five years, I've been thinking a lot about Briarwych, and wondering whether the church could truly be at peace. I was reassured over and over that everything had been resolved, but I guess there was a part of me that still worried. Now I've experienced the peacefulness for myself, and I guess I can relax now. Briarwych is at peace.

"Mrs. Lawley," the priest says as we get to the door, and as a middle-aged woman arrives with tears in her eyes. "Is there any news about your dear husband?"

"There's no change," she replies. "I thought

I'd pray for a while."

"Of course."

She goes through, and we watch as she makes her way to the set of pews right in front of the altar.

"Cancer," the priest says in hushed tones. "Such a dreadful disease. She comes two or three times a week and sits in silent prayer. I think she finds it rather comforting here."

"It's so different," I reply. "Before, no-one would ever have come here unless they had no choice. But there's really nothing here, is there? Definitely nothing evil, anyway. Briarwych Church is free."

A few minutes later, as I drive away from the village, I can't help but spot the church's spire in my rear-view mirror. While the future of the church seems settled, there's a nagging voice in the back of my head that reminds me I still don't know everything about what happened. In particular, I never quite understood why Judith Prendergast ended up the way she did, and how she became involved with Shaltak. I suppose I'd like to clean up that one final little mystery, but that's unlikely to happen. She left no diary, and there's nobody alive now who knew her or who was around in Briarwych back in 1940. So that part, at least, seems set to remain a mystery forever.

Still, that's something I can live with, as the

spire of Briarwych Church disappears behind the tree-tops and I turn my attention to the road ahead.

AMY CROSS

ALSO AVAILABLE

The Ghost of Briarwych Church
(The Briarwych Trilogy book 3)

The year is 1940. In the picturesque English village of Briarwych, Father David Perkins tends to his work at the local church. The shadow of war has fallen across England, and the local airbase provides a constant reminder of the horrors that have been unleashed. For Father Perkins, the struggle to provide guidance for his parishioners is an everyday battle.

And then Judith Prendergast offers to help at the church.

A faithful and devoted woman, struggling to raise her daughter Elizabeth, Judith takes a dim view of the happenings in Briarwych. Soon, however, she's offered a terrible deal, the consequences of which she doesn't fully understand. She tries desperately to escape, only to fall deeper and deeper under the spell of pure evil. And as she tries to set right her awful mistake, Judith sets in progress a chain of terrible events that will haunt the village of Briarwych for generations.

BOOKS IN THIS SERIES

The Haunting of Briarwych Church
(The Briarwych Trilogy book 1)

The Horror of Briarwych Church
(The Briarwych Trilogy book 2)

The Ghost of Briarwych Church
(The Briarwych Trilogy book 3)

Also by Amy Cross

The Devil, the Witch and the Whore
(The Deal book 1)

"Leave the forest alone. Whatever's out there, just let it be. Don't make it angry."

When a horrific discovery is made at the edge of town, Sheriff James Kopperud realizes the answers he seeks might be waiting beyond in the vast forest. But everybody in the town of Deal knows that there's something out there in the forest, something that should never be disturbed. A deal was made long ago, a deal that was supposed to keep the town safe. And if he insists on investigating the murder of a local girl, James is going to have to break that deal and head out into the wilderness.

Meanwhile, James has no idea that his estranged daughter Ramsey has returned to town. Ramsey is running from something, and she thinks she can find safety in the vast tunnel system that runs beneath the forest. Before long, however, Ramsey finds herself coming face to face with creatures that hide in the shadows. One of these creatures is known as the devil, and another is known as the witch. They're both waiting for the whore to arrive, but for very different reasons. And soon Ramsey is offered a terrible deal, one that could save or destroy the entire town, and maybe even the world.

AMY CROSS

Also by Amy Cross

The Soul Auction

"I saw a woman on the beach. I watched her face a demon."

Thirty years after her mother's death, Alice Ashcroft is drawn back to the coastal English town of Curridge. Somebody in Curridge has been reviewing Alice's novels online, and in those reviews there have been tantalizing hints at a hidden truth. A truth that seems to be linked to her dead mother.

"Thirty years ago, there was a soul auction."

Once she reaches Curridge, Alice finds strange things happening all around her. Something attacks her car. A figure watches her on the beach at night. And when she tries to find the person who has been reviewing her books, she makes a horrific discovery.

What really happened to Alice's mother thirty years ago? Who was she talking to, just moments before dropping dead on the beach? What caused a huge rockfall that nearly tore a nearby cliff-face in half? And what sinister presence is lurking in the grounds of the local church?

Also by Amy Cross

Darper Danver: The Complete First Series

Five years ago, three friends went to a remote cabin in the woods and tried to contact the spirit of a long-dead soldier. They thought they could control whatever happened next. They were wrong...

Newly released from prison, Cassie Briggs returns to Fort Powell, determined to get her life back on track. Soon, however, she begins to suspect that an ancient evil still lurks in the nearby cabin. Was the mysterious Darper Danver really destroyed all those years ago, or does her spirit still linger, waiting for a chance to return?

As Cassie and her ex-boyfriend Fisher are finally forced to face the truth about what happened in the cabin, they realize that Darper isn't ready to let go of their lives just yet. Meanwhile, a vengeful woman plots revenge for her brother's murder, and a New York ghost writer arrives in town to uncover the truth. Before long, strange carvings begin to appear around town and blood starts to flow once again.

Also by Amy Cross

The Ghost of Molly Holt

"Molly Holt is dead. There's nothing to fear in this house."

When three teenagers set out to explore an abandoned house in the middle of a forest, they think they've found the location where the infamous Molly Holt video was filmed.

They've found much more than that...

Tim doesn't believe in ghosts, but he has a crush on a girl who does. That's why he ends up taking her out to the house, and it's also why he lets her take his only flashlight. But as they explore the house together, Tim and Becky start to realize that something else might be lurking in the shadows.

Something that, ten years ago, suffered unimaginable pain.

Something that won't rest until a terrible wrong has been put right.

Also by Amy Cross

American Coven

He kidnapped three women and held them in his basement. He thought they couldn't fight back. He was wrong...

Snatched from the street near her home, Holly Carter is taken to a rural house and thrown down into a stone basement. She meets two other women who have also been kidnapped, and soon Holly learns about the horrific rituals that take place in the house. Eventually, she's called upstairs to take her place in the ice bath.

As her nightmare continues, however, Holly learns about a mysterious power that exists in the basement, and which the three women might be able to harness. When they finally manage to get through the metal door, however, the women have no idea that their fight for freedom is going to stretch out for more than a decade, or that it will culminate in a final, devastating demonstration of their new-found powers.

Also by Amy Cross

The Ash House

Why would anyone ever return to a haunted house?

For Diane Mercer the answer is simple. She's dying of cancer, and she wants to know once and for all whether ghosts are real.

Heading home with her young son, Diane is determined to find out whether the stories are real. After all, everyone else claimed to see and hear strange things in the house over the years. Everyone except Diane had some kind of experience in the house, or in the little ash house in the yard.

As Diane explores the house where she grew up, however, her son is exploring the yard and the forest. And while his mother might be struggling to come to terms with her own impending death, Daniel Mercer is puzzled by fleeting appearances of a strange little girl who seems drawn to the ash house, and by strange, rasping coughs that he keeps hearing at night.

The Ash House is a horror novel about a woman who desperately wants to know what will happen to her when she dies, and about a boy who uncovers the shocking truth about a young girl's murder.

Also by Amy Cross

Haunted

Twenty years ago, the ghost of a dead little girl drove Sheriff Michael Blaine to his death.

Now, that same ghost is coming for his daughter.

Returning to the small town where she grew up, Alex Roberts is determined to live a normal, quiet life. For the residents of Railham, however, she's an unwelcome reminder of the town's darkest hour.

Twenty years ago, nine-year-old Mo Garvey was found brutally murdered in a nearby forest. Everyone thinks that Alex's father was responsible, but if the killer was brought to justice, why is the ghost of Mo Garvey still after revenge?

And how far will the real killer go to protect his secret, when Alex starts getting closer to the truth?

Haunted is a horror novel about a woman who has to face her past, about a town that would rather forget, and about a little girl who refuses to let death stand in her way.

AMY CROSS

AMY CROSS

Also by Amy Cross

The Ghosts of Hexley Airport

Ten years ago, more than two hundred people died in a
horrific plane crash at Hexley Airport.

Today, some say their ghosts still haunt the terminal
building.

When she starts her new job at the airport, working a
night shift as part of the security team, Casey assumes
the stories about the place can't be true. Even when she
has a strange encounter in a deserted part of the
departure hall, she's certain that ghosts aren't real.

Soon, however, she's forced to face the truth. Not only is
there something haunting the airport's buildings and
tarmac, but a sinister force is working behind the scenes
to replicate the circumstances of the original accident.
And as a snowstorm moves in, Hexley Airport looks set
to witness yet another disaster.

AMY CROSS

Also by Amy Cross

The Girl Who Never Came Back

Twenty years ago, Charlotte Abernathy vanished while playing near her family's house. Despite a frantic search, no trace of her was found until a year later, when the little girl turned up on the doorstep with no memory of where she'd been.

Today, Charlotte has put her mysterious ordeal behind her, even though she's never learned where she was during that missing year. However, when her eight-year-old niece vanishes in similar circumstances, a fully-grown Charlotte is forced to make a fresh attempt to uncover the truth.

Originally published in 2013, the fully revised and updated version of *The Girl Who Never Came Back* tells the harrowing story of a woman who thought she could forget her past, and of a little girl caught in the tangled web of a dark family secret.

AMY CROSS

Also by Amy Cross

Asylum
(The Asylum Trilogy book 1)

"No-one ever leaves Lakehurst. The staff, the patients, the ghosts... Once you're here, you're stuck forever."

After shooting her little brother dead, Annie Radford is sent to Lakehurst psychiatric hospital for assessment. Hearing voices in her head, Annie is forced to undergo experimental new treatments devised by a mysterious old man who lives in the hospital's attic. It soon becomes clear that the hospital's staff, led by the vicious Nurse Winter, are hiding something horrific at Lakehurst.

As Annie struggles to survive the hospital, she learns more about Nurse Winter's own story. Once a promising young medical student, Kirsten Winter also heard voices in her head. Voices that traveled a long way to reach her. Voices that have a plan of their own. Voices that will stop at nothing to get what they want.

What kind of signals are being transmitted from the basement of the hospital? Who is the old man in the attic? Why are living human brains kept in jars? And what is the dark secret that lurks at the heart of the hospital?

AMY CROSS

Also by Amy Cross

The Devil's Hand

"I felt it last night! I was all alone, and suddenly a hand touched my shoulder!"

The year is 1943. Beacon's Ash is a private, remote school in the North of England, and all its pupils are fallen girls. Pregnant and unmarried, they have been sent away by their families. For Ivy Jones, a young girl who arrived at the school several months earlier, Beacon's Ash is a nightmare, and her fears are strengthened when one of her classmates is killed in mysterious circumstances.

Has the ghost of Abigail Cartwright returned to the school? Who or what is responsible for the hand that touches the girls' shoulders in the dead of night? And is the school's headmaster Jeremiah Kane just a madman who seeks to cause misery, or is he in fact on the trail of the Devil himself? Soon ghosts are stalking the dark corridors, and Ivy realizes she has to face the evil that lurks in the school's shadows.

The Devil's Hand is a horror novel about a girl who seeks the truth about her friend's death, and about a madman who believes the Devil stalks the school's corridors in the run-up to Christmas.

AMY CROSS

For more information, visit:

www. amycross.com

AMY CROSS

Made in the USA
Middletown, DE
29 July 2019